As the
Old Folks
Would Say

As the Old Folks Would Say

STORIES, TALL TALES, AND TRUTHS
OF NEWFOUNDLAND AND LABRADOR

HUBERT
FUREY

FLANKER PRESS LIMITED
ST. JOHN'S

Library and Archives Canada Cataloguing in Publication

Furey, Hubert, 1939-, author
   As the old folks would say : stories, tall tales, and truths
of Newfoundland and Labrador / Hubert Furey.

Issued in print and electronic formats.
ISBN 978-1-77117-609-5 (softcover).--ISBN 978-1-77117-610-1 (EPUB).--
ISBN 978-1-77117-611-8 (Kindle).--ISBN 978-1-77117-612-5 (PDF)

   1. Newfoundland and Labrador--Social life and customs. 2. Newfoundland
and Labrador--Biography. 3. Newfoundland and Labrador--Rural conditions.
I. Title.

FC2168.F87 2017   971.8   C2017-901021-2.
                                                            C2017-901022-0

PRINTED IN CANADA

MIX
Paper from
responsible sources
FSC® C016245
www.fsc.org

This paper has been certified to meet the environ-
mental and social standards of the Forest Stewardship
Council® (FSC®) and comes from responsibly managed forests, and verified recycled sources.

Cover design by Graham Blair

FLANKER PRESS LTD.
PO BOX 2522, STATION C
ST. JOHN'S, NL
CANADA

TELEPHONE: (709) 739-4477   FAX: (709) 739-4420   TOLL-FREE: 1-866-739-4420
WWW.FLANKERPRESS.COM

9 8 7 6 5 4 3 2

  Canada Council   Conseil des Arts
                       for the Arts   du Canada

We acknowledge the [financial] support of the Government of Canada. *Nous reconnaissons l'appui [financier] du
gouvernement du Canada.* We acknowledge the support of the Canada Council for the Arts, which last year invested $153
million to bring the arts to Canadians throughout the country. *Nous remercions le Conseil des arts du Canada de son soutien.
L'an dernier, le Conseil a investi 153 millions de dollars pour mettre de l'art dans la vie des Canadiennes et des Canadiens
de tout le pays.* We acknowledge the financial support of the Government of Newfoundland and Labrador, Department of
Tourism, Culture and Recreation for our publishing activities.

CONTENTS

The Great Chuckley Pear Debate 1
A Minor Problem 7
An Unlikely Hero 24
In the Woods 38
Outport Stakeout 44
The Art of Self-Defence 56
Thoughts on Resettlement 76
The Girl on the Veranda 79
Mrs. Maginity's Slapper 94
Men of Steel 107
Me and Sam 110
Revenge of the Fairies 130
A Social Visit 143
The Law of the Ocean 161
Feathers in the Soup 164
Tomorrow the Giller 179
He was a Miner 183
Across the Chasm 185
A "Noble" Spruce 213
One Small Book 225

Acknowledgements 231

I would like to dedicate this book
to my family—my favourite story.

THE GREAT CHUCKLEY PEAR DEBATE

It had all the ingredients for a lively, engaging, conversational evening, everything planned to perfection.

How could it be otherwise, when one is enjoying a delectably prepared meal with one's loving partner of thirty-five years, in the company of a gracious hostess and two lifelong friends, in a charming old two-storey house overlooking one of the most enchanting parts of Conception Bay? What could go wrong, you ask, in a setting veritably oozing with nostalgia and tranquility?

Well, something did go wrong, terribly wrong.

I can't remember precisely, but things took a negative turn somewhere between the freshly picked native Newfoundland garden salad delightfully seasoned with imported Coursada's lemon oil mist and the main course of baked Italian chicken and Catalan scalloped potato, sprinkled with just a hint of minced parsley. By the time the deliciously tempting Bo Taung Hoi lemon dessert arrived, the evening had thoroughly degenerated into something resembling raucous confrontation.

All because somebody mentioned "chuckley pears."

You wouldn't think anybody would be gauche enough to mention "chuckley pears" in such an idyllic setting, amid glasses of Cabernet Sauvignon 1972 and crumbs of LaTell de

1

Souce Artan French Bread! At home, in the confines of one's own indisputable bower—even in the arms of one's loving companion—one can talk about things like chuckley pears at length. But in front of an acclaimed academic! In front of people from another outport!

Well, somebody did, and the evening went from bad to worse. I mean, we could have talked about blueberries, for instance. There would have been absolutely no dispute about blueberries; no cold, darting, threatening looks, no violent arm-swinging in debate, no pounding of the table to jostle the crumbs of the LaTell de Souce Artan French bread.

No sir, there would be none of that about blueberries. Blueberries are easily discernible, easily identifiable. Blueberries could be our provincial symbol. Their bushes are unmistakably low, their berries unmistakably round and un-mistakably blue.

You never hear people argue about blueberries.

By the time the dessert was finished, the party had definitely soured. I mean, how can you eat delicious lemon-flavoured Bo Taung Hoi dessert and mention chuckley pears in the same breath? Well, the lady formerly from Savage Point who now lived in Little Cove could, and she was very assertive about her position—which women are supposed to be now that they are free.

"I'm telling you chuckley pears are small and round and black and fuzzy."

"Fuzzy," I affirmed.

I was on her side. Chuckley pears were small and round and black and fuzzy. Everybody in Savage Point knew chuckley pears were small and round and black and fuzzy.

"Fuzzy!" retorted her husband, a tall man from Little Cove who sat with his arms folded and didn't like the tea.

"Yes, fuzzy," his wife and I fired back in unison.

"Not fuzzy," interjected my wife. She was portraying disgust. Fuzzy reminded her of bears. She didn't like bears. She suddenly became very contemplative. "No, not fuzzy. . . . Bears are fuzzy," she added as an afterthought.

"But bears are much bigger," I protested.

"That's true. Bears are much bigger," affirmed my wife, now very contemplative.

"The definitive answer is right in here," interjected our hostess, holding the *Dictionary of Newfoundland English* over her head, enjoining us all, by that demonstrative action, to look in her direction.

". . . chuckley . . . a Cp various astringent in OED and DAE . . ."

"There, that should resolve it," she declared triumphantly, as she thumped the book on the table.

It was only her second glass of Cabernet Sauvignon 1972, but you could see she was definitely formulating a clear path to our enlightenment.

". . . choke cherry . . . choke plum . . . choke pear . . ." our hostess continued.

"Well, which one are they?" demanded the tall man from Little Cove impatiently.

"Which one *is* they?" corrected my wife, who is an English teacher.

"All right, then, is they," replied the tall man, smouldering.

He used to be an English teacher, too, but deferred to my wife, who hadn't retired yet.

"Well, it has to be one of them, doesn't it," replied our hostess, putting her fingers to her lips with a puzzled expression.

"Well, I'm telling you that a chuckley pear is bigger and pear-shaped and purple. I don't know what *you're* talking about," said my wife menacingly in my direction, "but it's not a chuckley pear."

My wife had suddenly vaulted from contemplative to combative, and I felt a shudder down my spine. I'm sorry, up my spine. I was getting very confused by this time.

"Aha!" shouted the hostess triumphantly, smacking page 96 of the *Dictionary of Newfoundland English* hard with her index finger. "Purple! . . . among the former were the purple chuckley pears. There. That proves it. Chuckley pears are purple. You're absolutely right." Indicating my wife.

"Definitely. Chuckley pears are purple," said the tall man, glowering at his wife.

"Purple? How can chuckley pears be purple?" queried his wife in return, formerly from Savage Point now living in Little Cove. Her face had taken on a look of total consternation.

"Oh, most certainly, chuckley pears are purple," stated my wife agreeably. "Everybody knows chuckley pears are purple."

She had turned to look stonily in my direction. My shuddering became an uncontrollable vibration.

"Black," I whispered. I was trying to rally, but it was all I could muster.

"Most definitely black," agreed the tall man's wife, formerly from Savage Point.

"Definitely not black," enjoined my wife coldly, with that if-you-like-her-better-than-you-like-me look . . .

"Why does it have to be purple," I implored.

"Well, it is," asserted the tall man from Little Cove, a strident tone to his voice.

The hostess still held her finger firmly implanted on page 96, her eyes darting from one couple to the other. Chuckley pears weren't supposed to break up marriages. They were small and round and fuzzy and . . .

"Purple!" exclaimed my wife, eerily reading her thoughts.

"Black!" I murmured, barely audible. The tall man's wife, formerly from Savage Point, nodded her head affirmatively in my direction, then sat erect, her arms folded defiantly in the direction of her husband.

"Purple!" grimaced the tall man from Little Cove, totally supportive of my wife.

Silence fell over the room. The hostess, feeling impelled to pour oil on troubled bushes, continued to read from the *Dictionary of Newfoundland English*.

"'Chuckley pears appeal most to the palate in the autumn, but it is in the spring when they are most beautiful . . .'"

Sullen silence greeted her cheery efforts. We weren't going to be put off that easily.

". . . when they are purple," glared my wife.

"Black!" hissed the tall man's wife, formerly from Savage Point.

"Purple!" snarled the tall man from Little Cove.

"Black!" I replied hoarsely.

Our hostess kept staring at the *Dictionary of Newfoundland English*.

She was secretly ecstatic. There was a new school of Newfoundland philosophic thought definitely emerging here. After all, Socrates had his hemlock. Silence reigned around the room. Something had to be done, and I had to do it. A brilliant idea suddenly appeared before me, a Newton's apple, a definite stroke of genius, a way to diffuse, a way to bring the conversation to another, more sociable level.

"Is a hert a blueberry?" I asked, my eyes brightening with a new-found enthusiasm.

Blueberries were as safe as the weather.

"A hert is bigger," glowered the tall man.

"No, it's smaller," glowered the tall man's wife.

"Definitely bigger," averred my wife in my direction. "And they're a darker blue . . ."

"But I thought . . ."

I didn't finish.

We talk about cloning now. Since they did that sheep thing in Scotland. It's perfectly safe.

A MINOR PROBLEM

Uncle Charlie Merrigan had a problem.

Well, Uncle Charlie Merrigan had several problems; what with the trap season turning out as poor as it did, the capelin being late, the cutworm doing the job on a lot of his cabbage plants. . . . Then, to top it all off, his only horse developing the "heeves" when the capelin did come, and he had the devil's own job getting a few capelin for the hay and the gardens.

But none of them could touch his latest problem, and it was a problem you wouldn't expect in the outport Newfoundland of the '40s.

The piano in the parlour played at the oddest times of the night.

There they would be, sound asleep, himself and Aunt Nora, when a thunk-thunk-thunk, slightly raised in crescendo with each note, would bring them to instant wakefulness, and they would lie there, alert to the sound, while the mystery player went the whole length of the keys.

Well, you might ask, and rightly so, what's wrong with a piano being played in the night, at odd or even times? And I reply, a lot, when you're sound asleep in bed and the doors are barred tight and you're the only ones in the house.

But before you ask why a piano in the parlour would be playing at the oddest times of the night, you might want to ask why there was a piano in the parlour at all at that time in our outport history, no doubt your mind being filled with all that rubbish about how poor and stund we were, and how we didn't have anything worthwhile to call our own and couldn't read and stuff like that.

Well, people in those times did play pianos and organs and fiddles and accordions and all sorts of things. Crippled Tim Wilson played the tin whistle like you'd never believe, and if you went to the right places, you could even hear a mandolin at a dance. And Uncle Charlie did have a piano in his parlour. Neither he nor Aunt Nora played, but he did have a piano in his parlour.

He had gotten the piano during the Depression.

John Thomas Maloney had bought the piano for his little girl Maria when he came from the States in the '20s—he had made a big bunch of money on the steel in New York—but when she died of consumption and he fell on hard times in the '30s, he couldn't bear the sight of the piano—it reminded him so much of his little Maria—and he wanted it out of the house. So he swapped it with Uncle Charlie for a calf because Uncle Charlie had a granddaughter, Sheila, who was taking lessons from the nuns and had no place to practise.

The piano stood against the wall across from the window and little Sheila would come in every day on her way from school to do her piano lesson. Uncle Charlie and Aunt Nora, when they could spare time from their chores, would sit proudly and listen as the little girl practised scales and attempted chords, all with a genuine child's enthusiasm.

Sometimes, on special occasions, like Christmas and St. Patrick's, the little girl would come just after supper, and neighbours would come in and she would play a piece she had learned, and everybody would clap and compliment her, and then she would go home before it got too dark.

Which explains the playing of the piano in the daytime.

Nobody could explain why the piano was being played at night, when, as I say, the doors were locked and everybody was in bed and nobody should have been playing the piano in the first place.

And not only *played*, but played, as I have already indicated, in a most peculiar manner.

It wasn't at all like Sister Mary Ignatius played at the nuns' concert, with that nice way she had of sweeping her hands up and down the piano, touching the keys ever so gently when she wanted a nice soft sound, or smacking both hands down hard to make a big crashing sound as a signal for everybody on the stage to bow before beginning the opening chorus.

No, there was none of that, to suggest that the piano was being played by somebody who actually knew how to play a piano.

There weren't even simple little melodies like "Mary had a Little Lamb" or "Row, row, row your boat." It was like, as Uncle Charlie would say whenever he met somebody on the way to the post office, "somebody was being tarmentin' with it."

Every night, with only slight variation, was an almost exact repeat performance of the night before.

The sound would begin on one end of the piano with a very slow thunk, thunk, thunk, then move very fast, the sound changing with each successive key, until it reached a tink-tink-tink at the other end of the keyboard. The last tink would be followed by a dead silence, sometimes lasting for an hour or more, then the playing would resume. This time the player would begin at the upper end of the piano, the slow tink-tink-tink increasing in tempo until the final thunk would again be followed by complete silence, a silence that would continue until the performance—if you could call it that—would be repeated the very next night.

* * * *

The first time it happened, Uncle Charlie came out of bed like a dolphin out of the water, and, confused as he was by the sudden interruption in his sleep, wondered why "the little one" was doing her practice at such an ungodly hour of the night. Aunt Nora, more alert at that hour in the morning, was quick to straighten out his mind and his senses on that point.

"For Heaven's sake, man, have a grain. What's the child doin' on the go at three o'clock in the mornin'. . . . Ye knows she's sound asleep in bed. . . . 'N ye knows every door in the house is barred tight . . ."

Because they had a big clock on the bureau that you could see if you looked right close and it *was* three o'clock in the morning and every door in the house was indeed barred tight.

They lay there side by side, listening intently as the crescendo finished, trying to make sense out of what, to them, was a very unnatural occurrence.

Not that they were terrified by silly superstition.

Sure, they were good Irish Newfoundland Catholics of the old sort who believed in people coming back after death and that sort of thing, but that wasn't particularly upsetting to their way of thinking. Such occurrences were, if you will, perfectly natural.

They never knew of anybody who had been hurt by a soul returning. In fact, everybody knew that souls only came back for a very good reason, and when that reason was taken care of—like the will being straightened out or whatever—the soul would return to eternal rest and nobody would be the worse off.

As they continued to listen in silence for whatever would happen next, Aunt Nora volunteered her opinion somewhat along these lines, her tone softly reverent, with no trace of fear.

"Charlie. I wonder if 'tis the little Maloney girl . . . comin' back to play on her piano. . . . Maybe she thinks it's still hers. . . . I wonder if we should give it back . . ."

To which Uncle Charlie gave a none too convincing reply, even to himself, because secretly he was thinking along the same lines.

"Tush, maid. Sure I paid for it fair and square wid the calf. 'N John Thomas didn't want to keep it. . . . 'N if she does want to play the piano again, she's welcome any time. . . . I mean to say, I wouldn't stop her from playing the piano . . ."

Although he silently wished that she would play it at some more reasonable time than when they were trying to get some well-deserved sleep.

They were about to broach another explanation for the strange happening when the descending process began and they both again became alert, straining to detect some clue that would give explanation to the mystery.

When silence again reigned throughout the house, Aunt Nora proffered a final direction for the night.

"After Fr. Mulcahy says Mass tomorrow, go right to the sacristy and ask for advice. See what the priest has to say. Maybe he'll be wanting to come and bless the house . . ."

Which seemed like a fitting way to terminate discussion on any problem, natural or unnatural, and they both rolled over and went to sleep.

The next morning they got up and studied the piano for some time, but there was no indication of any kind that the piano had been moved or damaged or in any way tampered with. Everything sounded the same when he touched the keys, and Uncle Charlie could only shake his head thoughtfully as he followed Aunt Nora to the kitchen, where she had prepared a nice breakfast of watered fish and raisin bread.

He sat staring at his breakfast and had to be prompted

to eat by Aunt Nora, his mind so totally absorbed with the problem. Whenever he looked in the direction of the parlour, he could almost see the little Maloney girl sitting on the piano stool.

But why was she playing in such a terrible way—if indeed it were her that was playing? Even little Sheila, at the worst of times, had never played as bad as that, and the common opinion in the outport was that little Maria Maloney, God rest her soul, played the best kind when she was alive. So it was reasonable to assume that she would play just as well after she died. No, it couldn't be little Maria Maloney.

"Now, Charlie," Aunt Nora interrupted in a concerned tone. "Put some butter on your fish before it gets cold. 'N don't let it muddle your brain. See what Fr. Mulcahy has to say, and we'll go on his advice."

He agreed to that, ate a hearty breakfast, as was his wont, then shaved and put on his white shirt and black tie and new coat, because he was about to discuss an important matter with the priest, and he had to be dressed for the occasion.

On his way to the church he met Master Curran, who was a few minutes late for school that particular morning because he had experienced some difficulty adjusting his new spats. Being of the old school himself, so to speak, Uncle Charlie doffed his cap to the teacher, who was a good ten years his junior, and then proceeded, without invitation, to offer Master Curran a full and complete account of the happenings of the night before.

Master Curran paused for a long time after Uncle Charlie had finished. Then he tapped his lip with his finger as he thoughtfully rested his other hand on his hip, the nodding of his head barely discernible as he stared into a pothole just at his feet.

When he finally spoke, it was obvious that he had given

deep and considerable thought to Uncle Charlie's predicament, and was prepared to demonstrate that he had acquired a deep knowledge of the piano, even though it was well-known that he couldn't play a note.

"Hmm . . . hmm . . . being played in a very peculiar manner, you say, Uncle Charlie. No sweet, delicate tremolos dancing softly in the whispered silence of the night, you say; no great elongated flourishing chords echoing their troubled resonance through the darkened stillness; no great thundering crashes for finales to signal the end of the composition . . ."

Uncle Charlie hadn't said any of that. In fact, Uncle Charlie didn't even understand what Master Curran was saying. Respectful as he was of the schoolmaster's vast store of knowledge, Uncle Charlie felt compelled to interject at this point.

"No, it's like he's goin' up and down over the keys."

This attempt to bring Master Curran down to a more intelligible level of conversation had some effect, although the appearance of deep thought still remained on Master Curran's face.

"Hmm . . . just going up and down over the keys, you say."

Here Master Curran paused, continuing in the same thoughtful tone.

"Tell me, Uncle Charlie, do you have a roller piano?"

Uncle Charlie didn't know if he had a "roller" piano. He didn't know what a "roller" piano was. He hadn't looked at the piano very closely. He knew he had an "Our Own" stove. . . . He could only echo the tail end of the question while he stared with some confusion at the teacher.

"A roller piano . . ."

"Yes," Master Curran continued, delighted at having finally arrived at the solution to Uncle Charlie's problem.

"A player piano. You know the kind, of course. You insert

the paper roll with the little perforations, and the mechanism inside plays the piano exactly as if someone were sitting on the stool. You can even watch the keys go down . . ."

Uncle Charlie blinked several times very fast in response. He didn't know "the kind" at all. He had never heard words like this in his life, and "perforations" and "mechanism" flew over his head like ducks flying south for the winter. Still, he was not an unintelligent man and, despite the size of the words, and the speed with which they were being thrown in his direction, he reasoned now that there could be a sensible explanation for the nighttime playing.

He tried to picture little Sheila playing as Master Curran repeated the particular features of the "player" piano—Master Curran mistook Uncle Charlie's attentiveness for not under-standing—but he couldn't recall any rolls of paper or anything like that. And she always had to press the keys down.

Unless. . . . He had seen Sheila's mother, his daughter, lift the top of the piano once to peer inside. Maybe. . . . He became alert once again as Master Curran concluded his explanation.

". . . So, if the mechanism became corroded or damp where you're so close to the salt water like that (Uncle Charlie's house was literally built over a beach), it's conceivable that a malfunction could have developed . . ."

Conceivable? Malfunction? Uncle Charlie was still sag-ging under words that hit like a spruce stake mall on a spring day, but by now he was getting the drift. Like I said, he was not an unintelligent man.

Something was wrong with the piano.

Master Curran, in the middle of all his "big" words, in-deed, in spite of all his big words, may have provided the solu-tion to his problem.

. . . If he did have a "roller" piano? A fact that he must now establish with certainty before he could proceed any further.

He did a true military about-turn at Master Curran's fourth "So you see, Uncle Charlie," and, without in any way complimenting the teacher for such a commendable performance, went straight back home to investigate this latest contribution to the solution of the mystery, forgetting all about Fr. Mulcahy and the sacristy or whether the house needed blessing or not. It was something that could wait, and possibly wasn't needed at all now that he had been given a more modern and more technological approach to his problem.

His hopes, to use the words of the more literate in our culture, were profoundly dashed. In fact, Master Curran's big words hadn't helped one little bit.

He didn't have a "roller" piano.

He and Aunt Nora carefully examined every inch and corner of the instrument and could find no roll of paper, and no place to insert it, a fact confirmed by his daughter, Sis, now that the story was out and everybody was turning up to take an interest.

"It's definitely not a roller piano, Pop," she had asserted, emphasizing "definitely" the way people in the outports do, and her assertion cast some gloom upon the couple, especially Uncle Charlie, who was now forced to re-examine his earlier thinking on the matter, one which involved speaking with the priest and trying to resolve matters that weren't as easy to deal with in the modern world.

So the very next morning, having heard the performance rendered on the piano yet again in the same disturbing fashion as the night before, he appeared before Fr. Mulcahy in the sacristy, holding his cap in both hands in a respectful fashion as he waited for the priest to remove his Mass vestments.

The priest carefully laid his alb on the sacristy altar and turned to greet the old man with a hearty smile. Fr. Mulcahy was a priest who truly liked his parishioners, and wasn't par-

ticularly alarmed when they failed to grasp the more demanding rules of the faith.

"Well, Uncle Charlie, what brings you to the sacristy this
hour in the morning?"

Uncle Charlie fidgeted with his cap a lot before replying.
Totally at home on the crest of a thirty-foot wave, he was completely lost in any kind of social situation that demanded this
kind of formal exchange.

"Well, Fawder," he said, bowing his head apologetically,
"'tis me piano."

The priest tautened somewhat in response, wondering
what lay in store for him behind the word "piano." The widow
Clarey still held it against him for not being able to fix her radio.

"Your piano, Uncle Charlie?"

"Yes, Fawder, it plays in the night."

Uncle Charlie was still fidgeting with his cap. Fr. Mulcahy
turned and began a little fidgeting himself, lifting the alb and
folding it a second time, searching for some understanding in
the pile of vestments arrayed on the little altar. He didn't know
how to fix a piano, either.

"Your piano plays in the night, Uncle Charlie?"

"Yes, Fawder."

At which point Uncle Charlie stopped, assuming that the
priest had sufficient information. Then he remembered his
conversation with Master Curran.

". . . and it's not a roller piano, Fawder."

Fr. Mulcahy had turned again to face Uncle Charlie.

"Not a roller piano?"

"No, Fawder . . ."

Fr. Mulcahy was still struggling for some kind of opening. He was hoping that this wasn't leading where it had all the
trappings of leading. If he had to confront one more ghost in
Miller's Bight . . .

Still, he knew Uncle Charlie well and was pretty certain the old man wouldn't come to him with some kind of cock-and-bull story. Then he was listening to someone who was considered, in his day, to be the best schooner captain that went to the Labrador from the harbour. He wouldn't come running to the priest with some silly haunted house tale, and would never make up a silly story . . .

He settled himself back on the edge of the sacristy altar, folded his arms, and decided to hear the old man out.

"So, Uncle Charlie, what exactly are you hearing?"

He let Uncle Charlie finish, pondering likely explanations as the old man provided details of the playing, then reached for his coat, indicating by his movements for Uncle Charlie to follow him. Within minutes the priest was leading Uncle Charlie back to the parlour, where they stood with Aunt Nora, surveying the piano.

"Now, Uncle Charlie," he said, "use your finger to show me as best you can what you hear when you're in bed."

Uncle Charlie hesitated to touch the piano, for fear that it wouldn't happen the way he had described it and somehow be seen to be lying in front of the priest. He was rescued by Aunt Nora, who was proud to demonstrate to the priest her ability with the keys.

"He goes like this, Fawder . . ."

She then proceeded to hit each key with her forefinger, beginning at the far left of the piano and moving as fast as she could to the right, hitting each successive key, until Fr. Mulcahy, having had a very tiring week visiting the half-dozen communities in his parish, and understanding very clearly what she was attempting to demonstrate, halted her performance at Middle C.

He had been following her finger studiously while alternately glancing to the left and right along the wall behind the piano, taking careful note of the two low tables that sat at each end of the piano. All he needed now was visual confirmation of what he was certain was the solution.

"Uncle Charlie, do you have a flashlight?"

"No, Fawder, but I got a lantern."

Before Fr. Mulcahy had the chance to reply that a lantern was no good—that he had to have a flashlight that could switch on and off—Aunt Nora had interrupted.

"Fawder, I'm always after him to buy a flashlight, but no . . ."

Fr. Mulcahy wasn't interested in being drawn into family quarrels that had their origins in outport culture lag, so he ignored Aunt Nora's admonishing tone, continuing to direct his conversation to Uncle Charlie.

"Can you get a flashlight, Uncle Charlie?"

"Yes, Fawder, Sis got one." (Sis was his daughter and the mother of little Sheila.)

"Well, Uncle Charlie, you get her flashlight and sit up tonight and watch the piano . . ."

This wasn't exactly what Uncle Charlie wanted to hear.

"Watch the piano, Fawder . . . ?"

The priest was unaware of the foreboding that was gripping the old man as he continued his instructions.

"Yes. Sit in this chair in front of the window. Sit very still and quiet with the flashlight off . . ."

"With the flashlight off, Fawder . . . ?"

Now, what sense was there in having a flashlight if you kept it off?

"With the flashlight off. . . . And when you hear the piano playing, shine the flashlight toward the piano . . ."

The priest paused before he ended with a tone of finality.

"You'll see the piano being played by . . . well, it won't be played by a human being."

". . . see the piano being played . . . ! But not by a human being . . . !"

That wasn't exactly what Uncle Charlie wanted to hear, either.

The priest had no idea that his particular way of expressing his thoughts was conjuring up the worst kind of feelings in the old couple's minds, feelings that became much more intense when Fr. Mulcahy did an abrupt about-face and turned to leave, suddenly remembering the sick call he was supposed to attend to right after Mass in Mackerel Cove.

"Just do what I tell you, and I promise, if the piano is played tonight, you'll know what is happening."

Aunt Nora clutched nervously at his sleeve as he headed for the door.

"Aren't ye going to bless the house, Fawder?"

The priest's tone was one of gentle assurance.

"If this doesn't work out the way I've figured it, I'll come back and bless the house. But, in the meantime, just do as I've said."

"Yes, Fawder," they both chorused, but the uneasiness was still there. And, if anything, the priest, as I say, seemed to have only made matters worse.

Fr. Mulcahy left them with some big, unanswered questions, questions that grew bigger in their minds as they continued their chores for the day and kept their minds from complete concentration on their work. They kept turning over the words of the priest in their minds.

"You'll see the piano being played . . . but it won't be played by a human being . . ."

The last part was particularly disconcerting if you thought about the first part with any deliberation.

If the piano wasn't being played by a human being . . . and you couldn't see . . . then didn't that mean . . . ? And he still didn't bless the house . . . !

It would be confusing to people younger than Aunt Nora and Uncle Charlie.

They said the rosary that night in an absent-minded fashion, Aunt Nora with her eyes closed, trying her best to imitate the holy pictures that were everywhere throughout the house, Uncle Charlie draped over a kitchen chair, very ill at ease, pondering the uselessness of what they were about to do, his eyes focused on the flashlight standing on the kitchen table, an obvious question recurring in his mind.

"What's the good of that bloody thing if you flashes 't on and you sees nuttin'?"

Then a shiver runs up his back as the next obvious question follows.

"But what about if you flashes it on and you sees . . . ?"

He didn't admit his fears to Aunt Nora over his nightly mug-up, and he was beginning to regret his decision not to take her up on her offer to sit up with him in the parlour.

"No, maid. Ye go on to bed. Ye needs yer rest. Whatever it is, I'll tell ye about it in the marnin.'"

So she had gone to bed and he resigned himself to the parlour chair by the window, the flashlight gripped in both hands and trained in the general direction of the piano, his legs extended in a slant to garner as much comfort as he could from what was otherwise an uncomfortably rigid position.

Unfortunately, unused to staying up after years of regular sleep, he dozed off, and the flashlight, which was supposed to be gripped and held in readiness, slipped from his hands and gently slid down his crossed legs, resting somewhere near his ankles. When the first thump of a bass key fought its way into his unconsciousness, he instantly roused himself, but he had to fumble for the flashlight, by which time the unknown form had leaped the scales, completed the night's performance, and, in effect, disappeared.

He was feeling rather shamefaced when Aunt Nora, awakened by the sound, appeared in her nightgown and housecoat, but she said nothing, understanding fully the toll the events were taking on her husband.

"Give me the light, Charlie, if 'tis any length of time, I knows you're goin' to be dozin' off again . . ."

She gently removed the flashlight from his hands, drew up a chair beside him, and sat to await the second part of the night's performance, much the same as if she were following an intermission in a famous opera house in some European capital.

They weren't long in waiting.

As soon as the first treble key was depressed, and a rather flat tinkle broke the silence of the room, Aunt Nora instantly flashed the light, to observe a small furry form hurrying its way down the keys toward the opposite end of the piano.

Uncle Charlie swallowed hard and temporarily stiffened, awaiting the appearance of horns and hooves and all the other eerie stuff that is supposed to attend happenings of this kind. But, of course, he saw nothing like that at all, and came out of it when Aunt Nora nudged him on the elbow, her voice carrying a tinge of laughter.

"It's a rat, Charlie."

Uncle Charlie couldn't believe his ears . . . or his eyes. He was almost let down. The explanation certainly didn't fit his expectations.

"A rat!"

He could hardly utter the words.

"Well, after that, never mind it . . ."

Which was the old people's way of expressing the incomprehensible, when the incomprehensible had to be expressed.

Aunt Nora was shining the flashlight back and forth in the direction of the corners of the room.

"Look, he's got a hole made in each corner. The piano is

right in between. . . . He hops on one end table, runs across the piano, then hops down the other end table . . ."

And sure enough, two large holes were plainly visible where the rat had gnawed through the floorboards. Well, where they were so close to the landwash, and you didn't have the concrete foundations of today, you can picture how it happened.

They used the flashlight to make their way up the stairs, Aunt Nora's gentle laugh accompanying them each step of the way. Uncle Charlie, not finding the unravelling of the mystery one bit humorous, just shook his head and muttered all the way to the bedroom.

"A rat! A baddamn rat! After all that, a baddamn rat . . ."

To which Aunt Nora responded in motherly fashion.

"Tush, Charlie. Say your prayers and get into bed. If 'twere something else, ye might be sorry for it . . ."

And when you examined the alternatives, any one of which might have been accompanied by hoofs and horns and terribly frightening things like that, a rat was as about as safe an explanation as you might want to get for a piano being played by nobody at three o'clock in the morning.

* * * *

I suppose the story should end there.

The mystery was resolved, thanks to Fr. Mulcahy, who didn't have to bless the house; and the little Maloney girl, we can assume, was happy enough in heaven playing whatever instruments are provided in that eternal sphere not to have the blame for the nights' interruptions foisted on her little spirit.

Uncle Charlie found the hole where the rat got in under the house and secured it, fixed up the two ratholes in the parlour, and the rat was never seen inside the house from that day till this.

But it was seen outside the house.

Uncle Charlie was down in the beach picking mussels at low tide some time later when he noticed a big rat, just like the one he had seen running down the piano, perched on a rock just a little distance away, eyeing him curiously. The rat seemed to have a big grin on his face, as if he were enjoying the fact that he had been fooling Uncle Charlie and keeping him awake all those nights.

Uncle Charlie, incensed at what he was sure was in the rat's mind, picked up a huge rock and hurled it in the direction of the form, while shouting the worst insult he could think of.

"G'wan, ye blood-uv-a-bitch. Ye couldn't play the piano worth a damn anyway . . ."

To which the rat must have taken instant and deep offence, since he disappeared behind the rock and was never seen or heard of again.

AN UNLIKELY HERO

He was an unlikely hero, sitting there on the end of the bench in our kitchen, quietly smoking a cigarette. There was nothing about him striking or unusual, nothing that would attract attention in any way, nothing that would differentiate him from a hundred other men of his time who had just stepped out of a fishing boat.

I remember studying him over the top of the book I was reading. He looked so ordinary, so typical of the men of his day. There was certainly nothing that would attract an observer's attention.

The way he was dressed was the way a lot of older fishermen dressed in those days: the thin, worn, visored cap sitting askew on his forehead; the heavy woollen sweater draping over the heavy, black, coarse pants; the knee-high fisherman's rubbers—black, of course; the red plaid shirt visible only by the rim of the crumpled collar and the edges of the water-sogged sleeves.

It was all too common, and could be seen on any harbour wharf along the coast.

His appearance wasn't impressive, either. He was too short for the thickness of his body, the heavy fisherman's clothes adding to the perception of an already too bulky form. His aging face, wrinkled and burnt red with the wind and spray of the open sea, was covered with a greying stubble, days old.

In the traditional mark of respect common to the men of his generation, he had removed his cap on entering the house, and it now rested inconspicuously by the leg of the bench, exposing unruly, greying hair. In its tangled and uncombed state, with patches flattened from the constant removing and fitting of the tight cap, his head gave off an unkempt, bizarre look.

My mother offered him tea and something to eat but he declined, stating apologetically that he had just eaten on his motorboat. Perhaps it were just as well. I suspected that he would probably feel uncomfortable—even a little intimidated—sitting in his fisherman's garb at a table which my mother always dressed as if she were entertaining the Queen of England, irrespective of the social status of the company. He may have been secretly aware, too, that his clothing exuded that blend of saltwater smells peculiar to people who follow the sea, and which became intensified by the searing heat of the kitchen stove.

As he sat he inclined forward, tilted so that his right knee absorbed the weight of his arm and the forward thrust of his body. This rather awkward-looking position enabled him to smoke with the least possible loss of energy or movement. The cigarette he held with the burning end cupped into the palm of his hand, to ensure that no ashes dropped onto the kitchen floor.

Everything about him was quiet, ordinary, nondescript, from the peculiar leaning position in which he sat to the rhythmic smoking of the cigarette. He would inhale quietly, then emit the smoke noiselessly as he continued to converse in soft tones with my mother, ironing on a table by the kitchen window. His conversation wasn't flowing so much as it was occasional; snatches of commonplace observations about weather and hay and gardens, to which my mother would reply in turn, her responses punctuated by the positioning of a particular piece of garment or the rhythmic motion of the iron in her hand.

Dressed for the cold and damp of the sea as he was, and sitting directly across from the big wood-burning stove—my mother always kept the heat at blast-furnace levels if the weather was the least bit raw—beads of sweat trickled down his forehead. He didn't seem to mind, however, looking comfortable in the kitchen and in the presence of my mother, who continued to iron and fold as she gave his conversation her full attention.

His grey eyes were expressionless as he gazed continually in the direction of the woodbox, pausing periodically to take short draws on the cigarette, emitting the smoke downwards, toward the floor, as if he did not wish to offend by his action. He straightened as he again explained the reason for his visit.

"Yes . . . all the way from St. Mary's, would you believe . . . then to break down just as we got on the net off the point. . . . Yes, break down just as we got on the net. . . . Clever salmon, too . . . we could see them. . . . Clever salmon. . . . We sculled in. . . . Granted, the wind was to our back. . . . Yes, you talk about it . . . all the way from St. Mary's and break down just as we got to the net . . ."

In the manner of his generation he would repeat words and phrases, as if in disbelief at the unexpected turn of events that had brought him into our kitchen. He spoke with the Irish lilt of the St. Mary's Bay people, like the people on the Southern Shore, in a soft, musical cadence. You could close your eyes and be in Ireland.

"It wasn't all bad, just the same. . . . We asked around . . . turns out there's a garage here. . . . At the head of the harbour. . . . So whilst the man from the garage was fixing the motor, I said I'd come up and say hello to George . . ."

He seemed to ignore the cigarette, the smoke curling upwards around his fingers, as my father's name took him back in memory.

"Yes, I said I'd come up and see your husband. . . . Hadn't seen him since before the war. . . . We worked together on Bell Island, you know. George and myself. . . . Didn't know he'd died, just the same. . . . Didn't know he'd died. . . . A young man, too, . . . God rest his soul . . . a young man . . . God rest his soul . . . a fine man . . ."

He shifted his position to lean back, drawing heavily on the cigarette as his eyes rested on me across the kitchen, as if something about me reminded him of my father. He continued his singsong tempo, speaking in a quietly respectful tone.

"Yes, b'y, I knew your father well. A fine man, your father. . . . You looks a bit like him . . . a bit like him. . . . Now, I didn't know he'd died, just the same. He was a fine man, your father . . . a fine man."

The latter phrase he would repeat, in a dreamlike manner, shaking his head as if he were having difficulty accepting the news of my father's death. Then he would lapse back into silence again.

My mother would periodically comment as she lifted or turned a garment, and he would respond, quietly, repeating a phrase, adding a word. Moments of silence interrupted their quiet exchange, moments during which his eyes would again focus expressionless on the woodbox, as if his thoughts were far, far away.

It was during one of these silent moments on his part that my mother abruptly changed the conversation. She had stood the iron on end and was folding a gleaming white starched shirt, nodding in the direction of our guest. Her tone suggested that she had suddenly thought of something very important.

"That's the man you should talk to, David, my son. You're always reading about wars. Mr. Mulcahy here went right through the war. Now *he* could tell you some stories."

"In the war!"

The phrase was rife with expectancy and excitement. I had been raised, nurtured, imbued with stories of Beaumont Hamel and German submarines off Bell Island. I had stood in the upland meadow as a child watching in fascination as formations of big warplanes flew over in the direction of Torbay airport on their way to strange-sounding places. I had sat just as fascinated at the edge of a card table hearing over and over the names of the men who were fighting and dying in those same places.

I had stood in front of the altar rail in our church a dozen times, reading and rereading the engraved names of the thirteen men from our parish who had died in the First World War, and I knew every detail of my uncle's death while serving with the Royal Newfoundland Regiment in Gallipoli in that same war. My head swirled with romantic names like Suvla Bay and West Mudros and Portianos Cemetery, where he was buried, at the age of nineteen.

I had followed the retreat and advance of the United Nations armies up and down the Korean peninsula, village by village, on a *National Geographic* map my aunt had sent me from Lynn, Massachusetts. And now, after two years spent in Memorial University—where I did my first real history courses—I was reading everything I could lay my hands on about battles and campaigns and cavalry charges. So, you can understand my excitement, at the age of eighteen, at actually meeting somebody who had been a real-live participant, somebody who had actually been there, somebody who had actually endured the horror and the carnage.

It wasn't the first time.

Our own little outport, like other towns and villages in Newfoundland, had sent young men and women to serve in the wars, and I had the occasion, at different times, to become acquainted with veterans and survivors, even at my young age. I once stood next to a sailor at a bar one Christmas Eve, reliving one of his Christmas Eve memories of 1942 in Walvis Bay. A man I saw day after day, a neighbour who lived just down the road, had been all through the North African campaign and took part in the invasion of Italy.

Yet these men would never talk about their experiences in the war.

My attempts to question or probe were never reciprocated with a like enthusiasm. The conversation inevitably became a pointless exercise. Their reticence baffled me, like that of my history professor, when I inquired about the scar on the back of his hand one day after class. He told me simply that it had been done by a machine gun bullet in an apple orchard and then he had continued on his way, as if, for him, that happening had been the most normal thing in the world.

My mother's suggestion had presented another opportunity to satiate my youthful curiosity on a subject that had come to obsess me, but when I looked up from my book at the man sitting across the kitchen, I experienced complete disillusionment. His presence conveyed only inoffensiveness and apology. He looked ordinary, just like dozens of others I had seen around the coast knitting twine or mending nets or just sitting on the heads of wharves looking silently out to sea.

The image he projected seemed of value only to blend, in some unreal romantic sense, with the sights and sounds of the outport kitchen within and the larger world of the seascape without, but had very little value for anything else. His conversation, to my newly acquired academic mind, was dull and uninteresting—references to news items on the radio, names of people sick and dying, talk of horses and capelin, of bad weather for potatoes and hay.

He didn't look at all like those young, athletic-looking

Americans or precisely tailored German officers that were the stuff of the war photographs that crammed the *Newsweeks* in the old press. I wanted to go back to the book I was reading, but I knew I had to be polite, so I dutifully followed my mother's invitation to speak with him. My question, however, betrayed no spark of my former excitement.

"You were really in the war?"

After his answer I would go back to my book. He did not have an inspiring presence.

He had to have noticed the disinterest in my voice, but he displayed no hint of displeasure. He just rested his eyes on me for what seemed to be a long time—thoughtful, kindly, understanding eyes that took no offence at the haughty arrogance of an eighteen-year-old university student who read a lot of books.

He took another long draw from the cigarette, then stood up and walked to the stove, lifting the damper before dropping in the butt. When he spoke, the tone was almost apologetic, the phrases coming slowly, like the gentle rise and fall of the sea.

"Well, I was in the war, I s'pose. . . . I s'pose you'd say I was in the war. . . . Now, I didn't jine up or go overseas in uniform or anything like that, like the other b'ys did . . ."

I tried hard to muster some enthusiasm.

"Did you go into Normandy, Sicily . . . ? Did you fire guns?"

He paused a moment before replying.

"No, I didn't go into any places like that. . . . I didn't fire any guns, either . . ."

He paused, seeming to recollect. The expression on his face changed even as the narrative took on a different tone, a tone I had difficulty interpreting. But the words were still quiet, inoffensive.

"No, I didn't do any of that. There was no guns where we were. Well, not on the boats I was on, anyway . . ."

Boats!

The word generated renewed excitement. Newfoundlanders by the score had enlisted in the Canadian and British navy.
I was so caught up in the word that I missed the part about "no
guns."

"Boats!" I repeated the word back to him. "You were in
the navy?"

He settled the damper down gently before he replied.
Softly, quietly, inoffensively.

"No, I wasn't in the navy. Like I said, I didn't jine up like
the other lads . . ."

He stood for a moment by the stove before speaking to me
directly, the words coming out factually, as if they were of no
great importance.

"I was in the merchant marine. You knows about the merchant marine, getting the ships back and forth. . . . Getting the
food over . . . the guns. . . . We never had any guns ourselves.
. . . Some of the other boats did. . . . Certainly, we couldn't fire
them if we did have them. . . . Where I was just an ordinary
deckhand. . . . An ordinary seaman . . ."

He returned to the same spot on the bench again. Then,
heedless of the fact that he had put a cigarette out only moments before, he took a sodden pack of tobacco from the
pocket of his sagging pants to roll another. But he didn't continue rolling. He just held the pouch in his hand, staring at it,
as if suddenly distracted.

"Just the merchant marine!"

The disappointment must have been evident in my voice.
I hadn't read much about the merchant marine. I did know
that they ferried supplies and war *matériel* across the Atlantic
to Britain, but they had never fought any battles or won any
medals. Then the story of the *Jervis Bay* flashed through my
mind; the story in our grade nine literature book about the

armed merchant cruiser that had fought the German U-boat to the end so that the convoy could escape.

I had never forgotten the picture of the captain on the bridge of his flaming ship, his broken arm limp, courageously going down with his ship.

"Was it like the *Jervis Bay*?"

I was still eager for an exciting tale. My mother continued her ironing with silent, regular strokes, pausing periodically to adjust a particular part of the garment. He removed a paper from the packet and shook some tobacco along its length before replying. He wasn't articulate like the professor.

"No, it wasn't like that . . ." He spoke very patiently. "Like I said, we had no guns. We just worked on the ships as they plugged along, trying to keep away from the submarines . . . trying to run away, if we could. We had to get all that stuff over there. There wasn't a lot of what you call action. No, we didn't shoot any guns or anything like that . . ."

I was starting to feel sorry for having begun the conversation and was looking for a way to end it. I became aware that my mother was looking up at me from her ironing, and I ventured on. I hoped my exasperation wouldn't show.

"But, I mean, if you went through the war. . . . Well, did anything ever happen. . . . Did you ever see a submarine?"

I was desperate for drama, remembering all those war movies, hoping for some small exciting tidbit of information that would satiate my original enthusiasm.

He seemed to be paying no attention to me, absorbed as he was in rolling the paper carefully over the tobacco. He then slid his tongue expertly along the folded cigarette, tapped both ends on the back of his hand to seal in the tobacco, and placed it between his lips. He hunched his body to one side as he rifled around in his pocket for his lighter, which he simply held at a distance, making no move to light the cigarette.

"No, I must say, I never ever saw a submarine. . . . It was hard to see a submarine. . . . Ordinary deckhands like us wouldn't be looking for them, anyway. . . . You'd never see them on top of the water. . . . Like where they came up mostly in the night. . . . And you'd never see a periscope . . ."

He paused as he closed the lighter and held it in his hand, next to the unlit cigarette.

For what seemed like a long time he looked far away into the distance, his face becoming very sad. When he finally came to himself and answered, he uttered a simple factual statement, almost an afterthought.

"I had seven ships torpedoed under me . . ."

My jaw dropped, but it was more a gesture of disbelief. The words didn't really say anything. Their significance contrasted too sharply with the plainness of the form that uttered them. The conversation up to now, like the person, had been dull, commonplace, without interest.

"Seven ships, torpedoed . . ."

I left the words hanging in the air, still in disbelief, completely unable to digest the abruptness of their content.

He took no notice of me as he continued, absorbed in the horrific memory, his eyes toward the distance. The words came slowly, sadly.

"Seven big ships," he repeated. "Seven big ships. . . . I saw a lot of good men go down. . . . A lot of good men . . ."

He was looking at the floor, his lighter again poised to ignite the cigarette which now dangled from his lower lip, his eyes still far away, his mind remembering. My mother continued her ironing with smooth, quiet, methodical strokes.

The shock of the statement, its sheer unexpectedness, had rendered me speechless. I could only stare open-mouthed at this fisherman, this very ordinary-looking fisherman, trying to comprehend the magnitude of the events the statement encompassed. It was simply impossible. I could only spew out senseless repetition.

"You were on . . . seven ships? . . . That were sunk . . ."

I had closed my book, and was paying closer attention, but exasperation had given way to skepticism. It was simply too hard to believe. He looked like he never left St. Mary's Bay. He must have been reading my thoughts.

"Yes, b'y. Seven ships. . . . Seven big ships. . . . One big tanker, six cargo . . . big ships . . . they all went down . . ."

There was still no offence at the disbelief that was etched upon my face. He just lit his cigarette and straightened, rolling to one side as he put the lighter deep in his trousers pocket, then patting the outside to ensure that it was really there. Then he became silent again, smoking quietly as he gazed past my mother through the kitchen window. It was just too much to grasp.

"Seven ships? . . . All sunk . . . ?"

It was the most inane thing I could have said, but I was having difficulty making the transition. It was impossible. Why would anybody . . . ? Was he making it up? He had turned to look at me again, deliberately knocking some ash into the palm of his hand.

"All sunk," he repeated. "All torpedoed . . ."

I could only stammer as the images pummelled my brain.

"And you . . . after the first one . . . you . . . I mean . . ."

I found myself staring at him, still trying to comprehend. I slowly counted seven ships in my mind, trying to appreciate the significance of the number. It was overpowering. I couldn't believe the import of my next words.

". . . you went back . . . six more times!"

His reply continued in that same simple, factual tone, as if it were supposed to be perfectly easy to understand. It was earnest, almost questioning, appealing to my rationality.

"Well, you had to go back, didn't you. You couldn't quit, could you! You couldn't let the other b'ys down, could you . . . the b'ys that didn't make it. You couldn't do that. You had to do your duty. Sure, you had to do your job, didn't you . . . like everybody else."

His expression hadn't changed throughout—matter-of-fact, straightforward, not able to understand why I couldn't. He drew more slowly on the cigarette, both arms resting on his knees. I sat motionless, grasping my book, unable to take my eyes off the weathered, bulky form across from me. I was trying to envision the seven ships sinking one by one: the explosions after the hits; the ships tilting and sliding beneath the waves; the frigid water of the North Atlantic claiming the dying, drowning sailors.

I pictured the man in front of me being plucked from the sea, again and again, oil-soaked and freezing and near-dead. And I pictured him walking up the gangplank of another merchant vessel, to sign on another ship, to risk his life one more time.

"Seven ships!"

My young inexperienced mind was fighting to disbelieve, to find something in the narration that could betray guile or deceit, something I could seize upon to point to the ridiculousness of the tale—but none existed. I found myself surrendering to the awesome power of the truthfulness that sat across from me, dressed in the everyday apparel of an aging Newfoundland fisherman.

Slowly, in the heat and smell of an outport kitchen, the silence broken only by the crackling of the burning wood and the continued rhythmic strokes of the iron in my mother's hand, my mind grappled with the inconsistency before me. For me, courage and duty had always come in the form of Hollywood good looks and neatly tailored military uniforms! But courage in the form of a windburnt face, bundled up in clothes that reeked of the sea, perspiring heavily and smoking a cigarette of cheap tobacco!

I would have to do a lot of thinking about that.

A light knock on the door roused us, and his companion's voice called to him from the doorstep. The motor was fixed and they should be heading back to their net. It wouldn't do to have the salmon left overnight. It would be "drowned" and they wouldn't be able to sell it.

He took another quick draw from the cigarette before again crossing the floor and depositing the butt in the grate of the stove. He then bent down and picked up his cap, grasping it firmly front and back and working it down over his head in an almost ritualistic fashion. He shook hands with my mother, holding her hand for a long time, looking at her. I could see his eyes moistening, but his voice gave no indication of the deep emotion he must have been experiencing.

"Your husband was a fine man, missus . . . a fine man . . . God rest his soul . . . a fine man . . ."

He turned to me to extend his hand in a gesture of farewell, his quiet eyes engaging mine. Perhaps he was remembering another young face just like mine, a face that his eyes had rested on, moments before disappearing forever from his sight in the heaving waters of the brutal North Atlantic. Then he walked slowly to the door, turning only to say "The best of luck to ye now" before edging his way through the porch and out.

I watched him from the kitchen window as he made his way to the wharf with his companion, both their heads moving in serious conversation. No doubt they were talking about horses or capelin, or wood or boats or salmon, how prices for fish were not getting any better. . . . I would have to look at those things differently now, to look beyond the ordinariness of the form, the everyday look of so many like him, to see the courage, the unshakable will, the loyalty and devotion that lay hidden underneath.

As he climbed down the ladder of the wharf, I wondered. What thoughts did he still carry within him? Did he think of stepping onto ships of death every time he stepped aboard his motorboat? Did he think of things like courage and supreme sacrifice, or did he simply go on—as he said—to do his duty, to the ones who never came back? When he looked at the ocean, did he still see the suffering faces of his comrades, burning or choking, gasping in agony before they slid forever into the silence of their icy graves?

He started the motor and stood at the tiller as he steered the motorboat out of view around the wharf. He had entered our house as a typical, ordinary Newfoundland fisherman, who, in the space of a moment, became an unforgettable hero . . .

Should I say an unlikely hero?

IN THE WOODS

The "gaps" are down, the ground is froze, the
    wood-paths choked with snow
Up in the dark to "tackle" the horse, as in the
    woods they go
Hay bag, oats bag, sharpened axe tied to a frosty
    seat
The grub bag has salt fish to roast, molasses
    bread the treat

Up the marshes through open "gaps," past hous-
    es still abed
Each man the master of the day, on catamaran
    or sled
With chirp and taunt, impatient click, they urge
    the horses on
Following time-worn beaten paths 'cross bog
    and marsh and pond

Honed cold steel of runners smooth make a
    harsh and grating sound
As horses strain with snorting strength to tame
    the frozen ground

The rhythmic beat of well-shod hooves from ev-
    ery horse and mare
Make music with the jangling bells in the frosty,
    steamy air

But there's no rush, there's time to talk, and yarn
    and gossip too
And pass the news, "tarment" . . . and taunt the
    laggard in the crew
There's many a laugh, a gibe, a joke, there might
    even be a song
(They wonder if Old Tom is ill, that he didn't
    come along)

On mornings when the snow is deep, and mount-
    ing drifts hold sway
The long trail in has to be cleared (they'll just
    beat the path that day)
So it's every horse a turn up front, and when Old
    Jack's tired out
Another horse steps in the lead, and takes his
    turn about

And so it goes, horse after horse have made a
    hardened road
A beaten path, made slick by sleds, to easy haul
    the load
But there'll be no wood cut on that day, both
    horse and man are spent
So they'll just mug-up in the woods and come
    back the way they went

Up in earnest the second day, and every day
thereon
Through the Druke, past Hick's Hump, skirting
Whalen's Pond
The Pinch is hard, and Suddard Point tests the
driver's skill
'Cross George's Marsh, along the track, to tackle
Saddle Hill

The way is smooth down the other side, with
Third Pond on the right
Past Merner's Knapps it's even ground with the
Snuff Box now in sight
One last marsh, one more hill, the Barrens yet
to cross
Everything's gone well so far, there's been no slip
or loss

The dawn gives way to daylight strong, though
the wind is fierce and cold
But at long last the Barrens end and they watch
the woods unfold
"Blackie boys" and old black spruce, "scaly varr"
and birch
"Whitens" for stove kindling, sir, white as the
painted church

So now they're here and it's down to work, in a
grove by Jerdan's Pond
And it's cut and saw, limb and haul, work hard as
the day wears on
No need to tether the faithful horse, he's got his
bag of hay

His oats bag resting close beside, he'll not go far
away

Most times they're cutting firewood, the driest
they can find
Then rails for fences in the spring, and stakes
that they can rind
Saplings made a picket fence, "lungers" to build
flakes
(Good "knees" for boat sterns will be found,
whatever time it takes)

In days gone by, they'd search for logs for house
and stable and shed
Everything came from the woods; every table,
chair and bed
Prime logs were taken to a mill, powered by a
waterfall
(In one small place the logs they cut built the
parish hall)

The morning's on and they've worked hard, and
it's time to take a spell
Axe and saw are laid aside when they hear that
welcome yell
"Now, b'ys, it's mug-up time, put the piper kettle
on
Get some water to brew the tea; cut a hole in
Biggin's Pond"

Wrap salt fish from the old grub bag, in brown
paper sapping wet
Throw it upon the burning brands—"No, it's not

ready yet"
The wet brown paper has to burn, then the fish is
cooked just right
(They just can't wait with watering mouths for
that first delicious bite)

While they dine the saucy jays will pitch right at
their feet
Chattering in their irksome way to beg a little
treat
What's left of the molasses bread will be their
midday meal
They're company enough around the fire, but
watch them close, they steal

A leisured smoke (they roll their own) perhaps
another tea
Then empty the kettle to douse the fire, they'll
want to leave at three
Back to work, cut more spruce, the load is not
yet done
Then drag and heave, and stow it on, to beat the
setting sun

Tauten the ropes with "bittensticks," no precious
wood slides out
"Tackle" the horse between the shafts, 'tis time to
be moving out
Horse and man attack the path at a much more
leisured pace
With a full load on, at the end of day, no need to
rush or race

Back at home, unload the wood and stack it in
    a pile
Blanket the horse in a welcome stall, there'll be
    supper in a while
Eat your fill, heave back a bit, then early "hit the
    hay"
At that time of year, except for storms, they'll cut
    wood every day

That's the way it was—"going in the woods"—in
    days now so long gone
They knew the name of every hill, every bog
    marsh, every pond
From the time the ice formed on the ponds, till it
    melted in the spring
It was "in the woods," hear the horses snort, and
    the jingling sleigh bells ring

OUTPORT STAKEOUT

Where Uncle Jim Donnelly hid his moonshine was somewhat of a mystery in Tickles. I mean, where it was illegal and all, it was important that it be kept well-hidden, especially when the Mounties were on the prowl day and night to stamp out what was nothing less than a heresy to that newly arrived mainland mind. The mystery was complicated by the fact that, no matter how much Uncle Jim made, or how much he sold to the b'ys in the wee hours of the morning, he never got caught with a solitary drop in the house.

"Yes, 'tis a mystery," the postmistress would say as she lent all her weight to yet another airmail stamp going to the 'States.

"Yes, a mystery," would adjoin the buyer of the stamp, as the seven pennies would be reluctantly counted out across the office counter.

And it was a mystery, a genuine outport mystery, one that warranted discussion every time the Mounties paid Uncle Jim another visit and came away empty-handed, even though it was well-known that the b'ys had been there till four o'clock that very morning "drinking 'er up."

"Sure he's got to be hidin' it," was Aunt Mag Maloney's certain conviction as she craned over the counter to scrutinize J. J. Mahaney adjusting the scales under a slice of frying ham. In matters of this nature, at least in Aunt Mag's mind, J. J. was somewhat suspect.

"Yes, he's hidin' it, to be sure," affirmed J. J., as he studied the reading on the new scales to ensure the correct weight. Given Aunt Mag's somewhat bellicose reputation, an ounce in the wrong direction could easily mean the beginning of an another outport civil war.

"Oh, there's no doubt he's hidin' it . . ." rejoined Aunt Mag, still scrutinizing J. J. with a distrustful eye.

After which Aunt Mag would say goodbye to J. J. and they would both return to more important matters of the moment, he to despairing over the mountain of unpaid bills left over from the Great Depression, she to the post office to garner all the news she could before returning home to cook the midday meal.

Even the schoolmaster felt it necessary to comment, using the words like "intriguing" whenever a less learned member of the local populace would broach the subject in his presence.

Not that anybody in Tickles really cared where Uncle Jim hid his moonshine, or indeed said anything the least disparaging about his making it and selling it. You talk about keeping the wolf from the door! In those times the wolf didn't dare come near the door for fear of being eaten on the other side. So you couldn't very well come down hard on a man who was trying to raise his economic status from nothing to something above that by selling a drop of moonshine on the sly now and then.

Besides, Uncle Jim Donnelly made the best kind of moonshine, as the constant trade to his back door after supper every evening testified. He was very careful about keeping his can and pipe clear of "vardygrass" (verdigris), so you didn't have to worry about anything like that—I mean being poisoned every time you took a swig or whatever. And his prices—at ten cents a flask—were, as they say today, competitive, in that everybody who made and sold moonshine charged exactly the same amount.

There were even those who claimed to have solved the mystery.

"He hides it outdoors in them bushes," was the solution advanced by Ritchie Nolan, resting his arms on an old, empty oil drum just outside J. J. Mahaney's store. ". . . Along that line of old stakes. We was in there one night 'n I was watchin' 'im through the winda 'n he went right along by them bushes . . ."

Being aware of the known character of the individual speaking, and his fondness for anything that came out of a corked bottle, the little group surrounding the drum did not greet this explanation with their usual show of comradely support. Marty Gull's response was an immediate snort of contempt.

"'N sure, if he were hidin' it under the bushes, 'n it were as easy as that, wouldn't you be lookin' fer it yerself? Wouldn't you be findin' it? Fer the love of the Lard, Ritchie . . ."

Which was a valid rebuttal when you considered the fact that Ritchie Nolan could sniff out a bottle of alcohol if it were wrapped in a squid trap and hidden under Long Point.

"I can guarantee ye he's not hidin' it where it can be seen," ventured Theophilus McCurdy, scuffing out a cigarette in the gravel, "that's fer sure. What with everybody cuttin' back 'n forth to the graveyard like that . . . 'n the Mountie's on the prowl day and night. . . . No, he's not hidin' it where it can be seen . . ."

Which they all agreed was good sense on Uncle Jim's part, since obviously anybody with a grain would never hide something where it could be seen.

"No, he's not hidin' it where it can be seen, but he's got to be hidin' it somewhere," avowed Marty, with the air of one who is convinced that he has the only possible solution to the mystery.

"Yes, he's got to be hidin' 't somewhere . . ." echoed Josie McCue.

In matters of this nature, Josie usually listened attentively and always agreed with whoever spoke last.

Ritchie Nolan shifted his position on the oil drum and the others focused their presence in his direction. Any movement on Ritchie's part usually precipitated perilous thought of some kind.

"What say we goes up tonight and buys a flask . . . 'n one of us stays well back 'n watches. . . . Say from a spot inside the graveyard fence. There's lots of spots ye can hide inside the graveyard fence . . ."

The idea burst upon the quiet of the afternoon like the brilliant discovery of that famous Greek man in the bathtub, generating stirs of interest around the drum, until the weight of the last part of the sentence made itself felt upon the circle of consciousness. The idea of standing alone in a graveyard for half the night was not one that was particularly appealing, especially to people who were not wholly convinced that nothing existed outside this mortal domain. For once Marty Gull was slow to respond, and he didn't speak with his usual tone of commanding authority.

"That's what we'll do. One of us'll stand inside the graveyard fence . . ."

His confirmation of the plan was followed by a second, longer pause, a pause ended by Josie's predictable echo.

"Yes, one of us'll stand inside the graveyard fence . . ."

After which he also settled back into a deep and profound consideration of Ritchie's proposal. Since Theophilus was the only one left to speak for or against the plan, they all felt that somehow he would provide the solution to their silent dilemma.

"B'ys, c'mon. What are ye 'fraid of . . . ? They's only a bunch of dead people."

His vocalizing of this realistic fact did nothing to ease the apprehension that had accompanied the articulating of the plan. Marty Gull snorted a second time, but not as vehemently.

"I suppose youse not afraid to stand in the graveyard, Theo?"

Too late, Theophilus realized he had been caught in a trap of his own creation. He wasn't that eager to stand around among headstones after dark, but he had brought himself to the point where the pride of saving face before his buddies now prevailed over the good sense in the head upon his shoulders.

"Sure, what's to be 'fraid of . . . ? They's all dead, ain't they?"

To which there was a certain quiet agreement before they all left for their respective homes.

* * * *

True to plan, the four b'ys met that night just around the turn before the graveyard road. Theophilus McCurdy was smoking his fourth cigarette in just under an hour. They huddled together by the ditch, speaking in hushed tones. Marty Gull had assumed the role of director of operations, and was whispering directions with the same sense of urgency as a platoon commander laying out plans to secure some close military objective.

"Theo, you go up 'round the back. We'll wait awhile . . . then we'll go in 'n buy the shine . . ."

Theo nodded his head by way of agreement, scrubbed out the cigarette he was smoking in the gravel, then proceeded to light another in its place. Marty, having once watched a war movie where the sniper shot a smoker every time he lit up, was quick to pounce on the foolhardiness of this latter action.

"Fer the love of the Lard, Theo. Ye knows he's goin' to be lookin.' 'N he's goin' to see that cigarette in the dark. . . . G'wan, fer the love of the Lard. Nobody is goin' to bite ye . . ."

Which isn't always the best kind of encouragement to have someone enter a graveyard alone at eleven o'clock in the night, especially when you consider the frayed nerves and jittery feelings that usually accompanied one's presence in that particular locale.

Not that Theophilus McCurdy was concerned about being bitten by those who came back to roam the world from their place of rest. In his mind they didn't have to go that far. All that was necessary for complete paralysis and an instant heart attack on his part was their momentary appearance anywhere in his immediate presence.

He edged his way toward the cemetery gate, trying to walk as quietly as he could so as not to attract unwanted attention from the other side of the graveyard fence, keeping his eyes on the ground as much as possible so he wouldn't have to look at the eeriness of the headstones silently reflecting the light of a full September moon.

He took up his position on the little rise inside the gate, the only spot where he could get a clear view of Uncle Jim walking along the bushes, trying to restrain the repeated swallowing that had become a constant part of his overall physical condition since he entered the graveyard. He stood stock still—his mother had once told him he made enough noise to wake the dead—and drew his collar up tight around his neck as protection against any untoward presence that would approach him from behind.

Now it was at times such as this that Newfoundland weather can become downright troublesome. The wind picked that particular moment to swing in from the north and shroud the cemetery in wisps of feathery ground mist, covering it with a vaporous blanket. Theo stood there, sweating and shaking, as damp shrouds and formless creatures slithered toward him, bent only on tripping him up and casting him down with the dead that rested beneath him. But he remained, too frightened to move, as tentacles of fog curled around his legs, cementing his feet to the ground on which he stood.

Meanwhile, the b'ys had strolled up the path to Uncle Jim's house, acting nonchalant and deliberately talking loud, as if Uncle Jim was supposed to know what they were up to and somehow be totally fooled by their actions.

* * * *

What happened next wasn't supposed to have happened at all, and would never have been anticipated by the b'ys no matter how long they stood talking and planning around the oil drum.

In accordance with the plan, the b'ys were supposed to request a flask of shine—which they did; Uncle Jim would leave the house to procure the flask—which he did; then Theo would see where he was hiding it—which he didn't.

Uncle Jim did leave the house for the moonshine, but he didn't head straight for the hiding place. He was shrewder than that, which explains in some measure why his stash was never discovered and why he was never caught.

He would always take what we would call today precautionary measures. He would stand on the back step first to have a good look around, then take his time walking toward the bushes, peering this way and that to ensure nobody was either watching or following.

That night he never got to the bushes.

In fact, he never got into the yard. His back door opened directly onto the graveyard, and as he stepped into the moon-lit night, his eyes alighted on a dark, motionless form seemingly suspended in the ground mist between the two cemetery gateposts. Theo, silhouetted as he was against the backdrop of headstones which sat silently on the hill, illuminated by the halo effect of a full September moon, the ground mist swirling about him in an ethereal manner, was, in effect, a first-class apparition.

Uncle Jim, whose nerves hadn't been helped any by being his own best customer all his life, reacted accordingly.

He stood paralyzed with fright, expelling what breath he could muster to utter what was intended as a prayer for his deliverance from the spectral form that hovered just feet ahead on the rise.

"Blessed and holy Mother of God, have mercy. . . . Blessed and holy Mother of God . . ."

This prayer must have given him a certain spiritual and physical strength, since he bolted back inside the house with a speed that belied his years, all the while pronouncing the same holy words as an unconscious means of controlling a very conscious sense of terror.

He stopped just inside the kitchen door and stood transfixed on the floor, white as a sheet, wild-eyed and trembling, trying as best he could, in spite of a dry throat and a good deal of sweating, to describe what he had seen, the telling being interrupted at intervals by the same earnest, repeated prayer.

"Blessed and holy Mother of God, have mercy. . . . Blessed and holy Mother of God . . ."

This induced added amazement on the part of the incredulous gathering, since up to that point they had never heard Uncle Jim say a prayer of any kind in his life.

Julia Donnelly, absorbed in her knitting, and totally unperturbed by the goings-on around her, was less than empathetic, since all she could offer was "Good 'nough for ye, drinking that ole moonshine all day long. Ye're liable to see anything . . ." although she did boil the kettle and mix him a big drink to steady his nerves.

Meanwhile, the combination of ground mist, head-stones, time, and cold were exerting their cumulative effect on Theo's mind and body, and the lights of Uncle Jim's house were becoming more invitingly comfortable the longer he stood on the rise. Then when he saw Uncle Jim bolt back into the house, the thought instantly entered his mind that the Mounties must have alighted on the scene, that another raid was in progress, and that perhaps he should get out of there as fast as he could.

He was helped in his decision by the appearance of a gigantic brown owl that had its nest in a birch tree at the end of the graveyard and which decided at that precise moment to investigate the strange, alien form that had invaded its territory. It swooped down behind Theo in complete silence, alighted on a higher gravestone a few feet to his rear, then let out a hoot you could hear across Conception Bay. Theo cleared the graveyard fence like an Olympic hurdler, and arrived at the main road with such speed that they say the owl is still blinking with astonishment.

Needless to say, nobody was in a hurry to rush out and, as the politicians say today, affirm or deny what Uncle Jim had witnessed.

So by the time the more courageous did venture through the still open back door, Theo had disappeared, the owl had flown back to its nest, and all that remained to greet their expectations was the quiet of the graveyard in the moonlit silence of the September night.

Uncle Jim ushered everybody home with a "No moonshine tonight, b'ys, no moonshine tonight . . ." which he repeated a number of times between intense bouts of chattering teeth, and the b'ys departed, none the wiser with respect to the hidden moonshine, but much more sober than they usually were on leaving Uncle Jim's kitchen.

* * * *

The rest, as they say, is epilogue.

Uncle Jim gave up drinking moonshine entirely, although he continued to make and sell it, and, as they say today, conducted a thriving business until times got better and everybody got jobs and it became the mark of success in outport life to display large bottles of rum and whiskey on small, newly purchased outport coffee tables.

The mystery of the hiding place was eventually solved, but not in Uncle Jim's lifetime, and you might say he carried his secret to the grave, or the graveyard, whichever you prefer.

Three years after he died, his son came back from Toronto to fix up the place and put a new fence around the property. When he pulled up the old stakes, he noticed that they weren't pointed at the end, like stakes are supposed to be. Then when he drove his first new stake, he felt glass shattering. He pulled up that stake, leaned in over the hole . . . and you can guess what he smelled.

"Well," he said, "I'll be damned. . . . The skipper was hiding it under the stakes. He was hiding his moonshine under the stakes all the time. Well, I'll be damned . . ."

We don't know if Uncle Jim's son was ever truly damned for happening upon the discovery, but sure enough, every stake hole had a full bottle of moonshine, well-hidden by the old stake that seemed to be innocently rotting away above it, testimony to the fact that Uncle Jim died with his boots on—or his brew on—again, whichever you prefer.

So the mystery, if you will, ceased to be a mystery, and the matter of where Uncle Jim hid his moonshine passed into that great oblivion of communal bad memory; and, except for the odd person who would be truly impressed by what was nothing short of an ingenious way of outwitting the world—and the law that was supposed to govern it—was rarely spoken of thereafter.

Not that the outport of Tickles dispensed with puzzling over mysteries. In that sense, outport mysteries are like useless "angashores." There's always another one waiting to take its place around the corner, and Uncle Jim's encounter with the unworld-ly visitor was seized upon with a relish that knew no bounds.

"Yes, the b'ys went up to get a flask, 'n when he went out to get the shine that's when he saw it . . ."

Which were the facts of the case as everybody saw them, and were agreed upon much the same as in a court of law, the explanations for the strange phenomena varying according to the individual speaking.

"'Tis his mother," averred the postmistress, "coming back . . . where he put her out that time and she had to go live with her daughter in Englee . . ."

"No, my dear, 'twas the widow Morris," countered Aunt Mag. "She wisht Jim Donnelly for all the moonshine he sold Bill Morris. They says that's what he died with . . ."

Even the b'ys had their theories, which they exchanged while they were standing on the wharf waiting to ship their squid.

This time Ritchie Nolan was sitting on a "gump" chewing a big wad of gum.

"I says he didn't want to sell us the shine. He caught on to something when he saw Theo wasn't with us . . ."

Marty Gull didn't agree with that.

"Naw. He musta seen the Mounties or something. Somebody said they was parked just down the road. . . . That's what I says . . ."

"Yes, somebody said they was parked just down the road . . ." confirmed Josie.

Theophilus McCurdy was more relieved than anything.

"I knows one thing. Whatever 't was, I'm some glad it wasn't there when I was there. That owl was bad enough. . . . Lard dyin', if I'da seen that udder thing I would've . . ."

Which sentence we will leave to the outport reader's imagination to finish, familiar as they would be with such experiences of their own under similar circumstances.

To date, the mystery of the strange apparition in Tickles has never been solved, and probably won't be—until they put a new fence around the cemetery or bring in really detailed weather forecasting or something, and then we'll have a perfectly rational and normal explanation, as befits our modern times.

THE ART OF SELF-DEFENCE

"So you're from Newfoundland, eh?"

The big man shifted his weight forward as he sucked in his coffee. The sneering, provocative tone was deliberate, intended to humiliate. He was addressing a younger man of much slighter build sitting directly opposite him. A husky man in gold-frame glasses and an attractive woman in her mid-thirties looked on apprehensively. They had witnessed their superior's badgering many times before and they didn't enjoy it; but there was nothing they could do.

Their superior was the editor-in-chief, and they were his unwilling partners in this all too familiar routine. The woman, the editor's private secretary, considered it sadistic. The husky man in the gold-frame glasses thought it disgusting, but he was not a man of confrontation and he had never learned how to deal with his superior's cruel temperament. The smaller man didn't respond, simply nodding in agreement as he fingered his serviette.

The big man continued, interpreting the younger man's lack of response as a display of weakness.

"Catches lots of codfish, I s'pose?"

There was a visible gleam in the editor-in-chief's eye as he mimicked the way he once heard an outport Newfoundlander talk.

Taunting Newfoundlanders about codfish was the editor-in-chief's accomplished way of demeaning them. He enjoyed their embarrassment. The tone was biting, intended to provoke, but the young man didn't react. He was peering intently into his coffee cup, as if there were something at the bottom he had forgotten to examine.

The editor-in-chief continued uninterrupted. He was a beast of prey toying with his kill, and he took malicious delight in tormenting the young, inexperienced writers, especially if they came from some obscure place in the Maritimes.

After all, the young writers were entirely within his power. And wasn't that what they were here for? Wasn't he Joshua P. Mackenzie, the editor-in-chief of one of Toronto's leading publishing houses? Didn't he have the power of life and death, so to speak, over every young writer's manuscript, over this young writer's manuscript? And, where this young writer was from Newfoundland, well . . .

True, he had read all the material that came across his desk, including this young writer's novel. Whatever the flaws of his bullying character, he was a good editor, and he had read the manuscript. It wasn't a bad novel for a beginner, and he had already made up his mind to recommend it for publication. But that could wait until tomorrow.

Right now, it was time for fun, and the young Newfoundlander, in the editor's scheme of things, had displayed all the right attributes of weak prey. He was friendly and open and had talked freely and trustingly about Newfoundland and his friends and family back home, to the delight of Mr. MacKenzie, who gleefully encouraged him for his own perverse purposes. Now that the young writer had been softened up with light conversation over a three-course dinner in one of the finest restaurants in Toronto, the games could begin. This was going to be easy: too easy, too one-sided, no challenge.

"Mr. Mackenzie . . . !" His secretary's tone was entreating, pleading.

She wanted her superior to stop the baiting before it began. She was from a small town in Nova Scotia and had experienced it herself: the witty insults, the undeserved embarrassment, the sense of powerlessness. Being sensitive by nature, she empathized with these young, beginning writers, but she knew she could not help. The editor-in-chief was simply too overpowering—and he was her boss. Anyway, she knew that once the tormenting began it would not end until the potential victim had been reduced to a state of total humiliation.

She exchanged helpless glances with the assistant editor in the gold-rimmed glasses, but the latter simply shrugged and slouched back helplessly. In spite of his accomplished—and superior—intellect, and the fact that he, like the editor-in-chief, was from Toronto, he knew he was no match for his brutish boss at this level of confrontation. He could only offer silent emotional support.

"They gives honorary doctorates to the ones who cuts open the most codfish, I s'pose," the editor-in-chief continued in his mimicking tone, winking in the direction of the assistant editor. He was alluding to the granting of that prestigious honour to the first premier of Newfoundland. The assistant editor did not acknowledge the wink. The young writer still didn't respond. He was studiously turning the coffee cup from back to front, totally engrossed in its movement.

The two assistants looked imploringly at Mr. Mackenzie, but he ignored them. He had the young writer where he wanted him, to where he had reduced so many before, to that state of abject confusion, where they were too intimidated, too destroyed, to reply.

"I heard you haves to work with lots of fish guts in your

university there, what's its name . . . oh, yes, Memorial . . . before you gets your degree."

The editor-in-chief knew enough about the culture to frame the insult. He wasn't unintelligent. The tone was more gleeful. Disposing of the fish entrails, the guts and sound bones, was considered by him as working in dirt, subhuman, degrading. It was intended to hurt.

He had moved his body so that he was leaning directly forward, his thick torso and bushy head with its apelike eyebrows dominating the little group. This position was his most imposing, his most formidable, his most dangerous, as he continued the mocking tone.

"What I can't understand is how you gets the smell of fish off the degree before you hangs it on the wall; but I s'pose the kinds of houses you hangs it in, it don't make no difference."

With this taunt, the badgering seemed to have worked. The Newfoundlander repositioned himself and looked around the table. Astonishingly, his air was surprisingly casual, unperturbed. He had set the coffee cup gently in the saucer and was resting his arm on the table, where his finger traced some unintelligible pattern on the serviette. His other arm rested loosely on his leg. In the slouching position he had assumed, he looked totally nonplussed.

The two assistants sat with their eyes downcast. The young Newfoundlander inhaled deeply and made a peculiar movement with his jaw, clicking his teeth as if he were trying hard to remember something. He looked directly into the eyes of his tormentor before he finally spoke, in a subdued, even tone.

"As a matter of fact, I never caught a fish in my life."

He didn't say "codfish." He just said "fish," like Newfoundlanders do.

"A Newfoundlander who never caught a fish! You're putting me on."

The editor-in-chief guffawed. He seemed genuinely incredulous.

"Never caught a fish!" he repeated, studying the young writer with amusement. "So what did you do for money . . . for all that university?"

Here he leaned back, nodding his head in mock understanding.

"Oh, I know. Our unemployment insurance. All the money we send you from Ottawa. You gets your stamps . . ."

The editor-in-chief's voice trailed off, delighted with his response. The secretary and the assistant editor winced. The taunting had become too excessive, too belligerent, but the editor continued, his face bland of emotion, his demeaning tone cloaked in a feigned sincerity, as if he were truly interested.

"So, with all that squalor and welfare, how did you do it? Get through university, I mean? All those degrees you have . . ."

He rested his thick elbows on the table, relaxing in the knowledge of his superiority.

"They're not honorary, are they? Of course they wouldn't be, would they? You'd have to be a little prime minister with a big bow tie to get the honorary ones, wouldn't you?"

It was another derisive reference to Newfoundland's first prime minister. This man was a master. He was in control, pushing, probing, exploring the terrain, looking for a weakness.

"You must have worked at something," he insisted, his expression one of mock exasperation. You fellows never have any money, do you . . . except what you get from us, of course?"

His eyes were gleaming again. This writer had to break soon. None of them held out this long. The young Newfoundlander continued to look straight at his tormentor. Nothing about him had changed. When he spoke he seemed unaffected by the harassment. The taunting, the debasing tone, seemed never to have happened. His response continued to be even, controlled.

"Yes, I did work, no question about that. I had to, like a lot of others from the outports."

He used the traditional Newfoundland word for the many tiny villages that clung precariously to the rocks around the Newfoundland coastline.

"None of us had very much, like you say. Although we weren't as bad off as you're making us out to be, like you read about in those other countries. Still, if you wanted to get anywhere, you had to work hard."

He sat straight up, warming to his own defence, but he was still casual, almost nonchalant in his tone.

"We were never hungry, though, just the same . . . we had lots of rough grub . . . and we were always warm. But we didn't have much money, cash money . . . I've got to agree with you there."

He stopped, as if finished with his defence, seemingly satisfied with his explanation. He reached for his wineglass, which was still full, and raised it to his lips, going through the motion of sipping, though no wine left the glass. His eyes had taken on a peculiar cast, as if he were seeing again what he had left behind, and was proud of the memory.

The editor-in-chief paused, unable to comprehend a new turn of mood which had somehow come to dominate the table, although he didn't immediately show it. Something about this young writer was beginning to unnerve him, as if he were becoming aware for the first time of some impenetrable shield that encased the young man's presence, a shield that defied every one of his satiric barbs, a shield that hid something deep and cautioning.

This writer wasn't responding like the others. He should have been broken by this time. His position as editor-in-chief, his control over any attempt at publication, his intimidatory presence should have forced the writer to cow to his sadistic game playing, to succumb to his indefatigable bullying. It should have been over by now, but it was like it hadn't even begun.

This Newfoundlander was perplexing him. Worse, it was disturbing him. He had seemed so easy to figure out in the beginning—youthful, naive, gullible, easy to manipulate—but he was now displaying a mysterious strength, and the game was not unfolding the way the editor had planned. Something in the tone of the young writer's replies just didn't fit. Something hard and flintlike was forming behind those eager, open eyes; something hard and flintlike that could only be noticed if the observer were very astute; something hard and flintlike that warned of danger to any who came too close, who tried to penetrate the shield too deeply.

The secretary and the assistant had noticed something, too, and they both turned to study the young writer, but they still didn't understand. They too were puzzled by his failure to break.

"No, I didn't fish at all," the young writer repeated. "In fact, none of my family fished. They were all ironworkers. My father, my uncles, my brothers, all my cousins—just about everybody where I come from—all worked at the steel, putting up those big buildings . . ."

He continued to look at the editor-in-chief as he absentmindedly toyed with the full glass of wine that now rested on the table.

". . . New York, Boston, Philadelphia, places like that. Oh, we might have caught a fish or two in the fall of the year, enough for the winter, if you know what I mean, but we wouldn't call ourselves fishermen. We weren't fishermen, like them fellas in Englee and Bonavista . . . and them places."

He was slipping into his outport way of speaking, with which he seemed more at ease. He stopped to raise the wine-glass to his lips but he still didn't take any wine, and he didn't continue. The editor sat back uneasily. The others waited. The assistant editor spoke for the first time, relieved by the new turn in the conversation.

"So you were an ironworker? That's how you put yourself through."

The assistant editor was always sincerely interested in the young writers, and they liked him. He was easy with them, and he had character. The young Newfoundlander turned toward him, his eyes softening. When he spoke, his voice was tinged with laughter.

"Me, an ironworker? No way. I couldn't climb for beans. I mean, have you ever seen those fellows climb steel—eighty, ninety, a hundred stories up, walking on steel beams inches wide . . . ? No sir, you'd never get me up there in a month of Sundays. Me for good old solid ground. If I'm going to fall, it's going to be from right here."

He nodded his head downwards as he indicated a distance from the floor with the palm of his hand.

"So, what did you do?" asked the secretary, following his movement with interest.

"Like you said, you didn't have much, and you put your-self through all those years of university. You have a couple of degrees, don't you?"

The young man nodded in the affirmative.

"So, how did you earn money?" she continued.

It was a sincere question, in a respectful tone. The young writer perused her before answering, his eyes rest-ing softly upon the openness and honesty in her expres-sion. Then he shifted his position to look directly at the editor-in-chief, responding with a casualness that seemed out of place with the words, words that seemed paced for effect.

"I was, what they call in New York . . ." and here he hesitated, pronouncing the words almost with disinterest, ". . . a street-fighter."

He raised the wineglass again to his lips, holding the glass in that position for a long time, although he still didn't sip any wine. He rotated the glass slowly in the light before setting it back on the table.

The assistant editor and the secretary exchanged surprised glances, unable to reconcile the implications of the statement with the quiet personality they had come to know, even in such a short time. The editor-in-chief sat immobile, the look on his face hovering between scorn and incredulity, but the colour of his face changed slightly, and a tinge that looked like fear flickered momentarily in his eyes.

The tinge, however, just as rapidly disappeared, as he fell back into his bullying disposition, acutely aware of the contrast between the words and the person who had uttered them. The words that conjured up images of viciousness and savagery simply did not match the inoffensive-looking person who sat across from him. It was too much to accept. Still, he didn't sound quite as sure of himself as before, even as he snorted a contemptuous response.

"You, a street-fighter! I've seen street-fighters. They're as hard as they look. You look like a cream puff. They'd eat you for breakfast."

He was trying to snarl but it didn't quite come off. He had become inexplicably wary, apprehensive. His arrogance had waned and his eyes were troubled. His physical size and the overpowering strength of his position had never been challenged before, and this young writer was challenging him: quietly, subtly, and it continued to unnerve him, rendering him more and more uncomfortable. Like all insecure, bullying people, he could only equate strength with size.

He would have liked to dismiss the person across from him as puny, weak, inconsequential, to dismiss him with a contemptuous wave of his huge bearlike hand, but something in the young writer's tone, something in the way he was now controlling the conversation, was inducing a tightness in the editor-in-chief's stomach. When their eyes met, he involuntarily swallowed as if a lump were in his throat.

He had picked up the hard flint in the writer's eyes again.

"You, a street-fighter," echoed the secretary, her voice resounding in the silent interval. Reared in a quiet country town in Nova Scotia, she had never witnessed any kind of a physical confrontation in her life, but she had watched Mafia movies with her boyfriend, and she knew what a tough guy was supposed to look like.

"Aren't they tough-looking and all scarred up?"

She shook her head in disbelief, contrasting him with the movie image. In her mind, he just didn't stack up at all.

"You're putting us on," enjoined the assistant editor, studying the young writer intently. A wry smile was slowly forming on his face.

"You . . . well . . . you just don't look the part."

He emphasized "look," as his eyes appraised the slight build of the man who was the focus of his attention.

The young writer ignored their looks as he gazed intently at the full wineglass which he still held in his hand, seemingly unaffected by the surprise and disbelief which had greeted his announcement, as if it were exactly the kind of response he should have expected.

When he raised his eyes to speak, his tone was assuring.

"Well, you can believe it," he said. "For all those years I attended university I paid my way as a street-fighter. Of course, they didn't call it that in Newfoundland," he said, looking quickly from one to the other of his small audience. "They didn't have any streets then."

Here he stopped and smiled in the direction of Mr. Mackenzie. His tone had resumed its buoyancy, his eyes were again light and cheery.

"So, where did you fight?" The assistant editor was curious. "I mean, if you didn't fight on the street, and I don't mean to infer . . ."

He coloured a little when he thought of the hidden meaning of his question, which was unintended. The writer continued on, taking no notice of the assistant editor's look of embarrassment.

"You're right, we didn't fight on the street—or on the road, for that matter. As far as the old people were concerned, only the 'rals' did that. I mean, the punks, the real thugs. Any Newfoundlander who was a gentleman would challenge you to the public wharf and you'd have it out in fair play, shake hands when it was over, and go back to whatever you were doing—win, lose, or draw. That's the way the old people fought."

A sense of pride was evident in his voice. He was talking about his people. He leaned forward to pick up the serviette but seemed to change his mind.

"Anyway, by the time I was getting old enough to do that stuff, we were in Confederation and it was called creating a disturbance, disturbing the peace, or whatever, and you could get arrested by the RCMP, the new police force."

"But, you must have fought somewhere. Where did you fight?" the exasperation was evident in the secretary's voice.

"Well, I told you I came from an ironworker background. I just chased the job sites. Mostly across the Gulf . . . the big cities . . . wherever the buildings were going up, wherever there were ironworkers," he replied in her direction. "That's where

I'd head. Any job site was good for business. These ironworkers were hard as nails. There weren't many who didn't like a good scrap—or watch one—and it wasn't hard to line up somebody for a good fight. You could always count on a couple of fights even on the smallest job."

He reached for the serviette a second time, then just as mysteriously refrained from touching it, continuing in a matter-of-fact tone of voice.

"My second cousin, who was my manager of sorts, would scout out the place a day or two before, determine whether anybody was interested, who could be talked into a betting fight, set up the odds, that sort of thing. He had spent a few years on the streets in New York and he knew the ropes on the street-fighting routine, if you don't mind the pun."

He stopped, somewhat abashed at having drawn attention to his play on words. Nobody else had noticed. The assistant editor and the secretary were listening attentively. Only the editor-in-chief seemed uncomfortable. He had become visibly more unnerved. The young writer gave him a passing glance as he continued.

"So he would line everything up, and I would turn up a day or two later, do the fights, collect the winnings, and we'd both be on our way to the next job site."

"Collect the winnings! You! Win!" The editor-in-chief snorted again.

"How could you win? Like I said, you look like a cream puff. And these ironworkers are as hard as the steel they put up."

He was using the same snorting tone, but it sounded vapid and empty, and his composure seemed shaken.

The Newfoundlander accepted the reprobation gracefully. Only his eyes showed any response to the harshness of the tone. They had become as hard as steel. He picked up the folded serviette, examining it carefully before tucking it under the edge of a saucer. He leaned closer to the group as he spoke, his voice becoming matter-of-fact.

"What you're saying is that I look like I can't fight my way out of a wet paper bag. That's how they'd say it back home," he added, nodding his head in agreement with the editor-in-chief. ". . . And you're absolutely right. That's exactly how I look."

The wineglass was again in his hand, and for the first time he took a long, slow sip of red wine, his eyes never leaving the form of the editor-in-chief as he leaned back, carefully resting the wineglass on the table. He pronounced the next sentence with a half-smile, the look on his face one of quiet satisfaction. He seemed to be savouring the memories of triumph and victory.

"That's exactly how I won all the money."

He stressed "exactly." Then he leaned forward again, as if to speak in confidence, adopting a seriously questioning tone.

"Would you bet on me? I mean, one look at me and the guys on the job would split their sides laughing."

He leaned back, satisfied that his question had achieved its intent.

"That's how I made my money. Nobody ever bet on me— nobody. And I can tell you"—here he leaned forward again, his hand held high over the table—"the odds were always this high."

The editor-in-chief's eyes narrowed. He was swallowing hard and the tightness was increasing in his stomach.

"What kind of a fighter were you?" the assistant editor queried, his eyes still portraying doubt. "Did you do any of that karate stuff . . . judo, boxing?"

The young writer eased back, relaxed in his response.

"No, I wasn't polished like that. That's what we'd call 'fancy' fighting back home. You must remember I grew up in an outport in Newfoundland, and there was no way to learn anything like that in a Newfoundland outport. The good fighters were natural-born fighters. You couldn't learn that, and I never did."

The assistant editor continued in a mildly curious tone.

"But you must have learned how to fight somewhere . . . in order to win like you did. . . . You weren't a natural-born fighter. You weren't trained . . ."

The secretary had been trying to interject for some time. The young writer met her eyes again. His voice was factual.

"Well, actually, I was trained. . . . Not in karate or anything like that. . . . But I was trained . . . and trained very well."

Here the young writer again toyed with the serviette as he waited for the words to take effect."

"Trained? How? You said you didn't . . ."

The secretary seemed on the point of complete exasperation. The young writer picked up the serviette and tossed it toward the centre of the table with a dramatic motion, his eyes surveying the group.

"The military. The Airborne Division. . . . In it for three years. And let me tell you, them fellas train you. . . . It's not fancy or anything like that, but there's not much left of the other fella when you're finished with him. . . . I can tell you that. . . . Yes sir, they turn you into one hell of a killer . . ."

The words were relaxed in tone, tossed out nonchalantly, but it made the editor-in-chief start. The writer continued, still casually narrating.

"You must have heard about the British commandos . . . Second World War. You know how hard they were trained. Well, my son, the Airborne makes them look like pussycats. And as far as street-fighting is concerned, the Airborne makes that stuff look like fun . . . compared to the stuff we learned . . ."

He paused before looking straight at the editor-in-chief.

"'Get them any way you can' was our motto. Kill or be

killed, exactly as if you were on the front lines. Yes sir, kill or be killed."

He reached for his wineglass as he calmly surveyed the looks of horror that greeted his last statement. He continued into the stunned silence as he again looked directly at the editor-in-chief.

"I was a pussycat before I joined the Airborne, but I tell you I had no trouble after I finished. I didn't want to stay with the military. There really wasn't anything else I wanted to do except go to university, so I got into using my training to make a dollar, as they say. Well, actually, it was my cousin who came up with the idea, after he saw me work over that guy in the bar, and sort of became my manager . . . for a cut, naturally."

"The guy in the bar?" The secretary's face was frozen in horror.

The young writer never deviated from his casual tone. He could have been telling them how he rowed boats back and forth across the harbour.

"Yeah. Called me a stupid so-and-so of a Newf. Sir, by the time I was finished with him, he couldn't say too many words. Jaw stomped to pieces, teeth all over the floor. . . . Smashed ribs, punctured spleen . . . from the boots, you know . . . you couldn't see his face. By the time they hauled me off, he wasn't very pretty. . . . Don't know if he ever got out of hospital . . ."

The young writer took a large sip of wine and set the glass gently on the table, as if he were finished with the conversation.

The assistant editor caught the look of horror on the secretary's face and seemed anxious to change the tone of conversation. The editor-in-chief sat motionless, his eyes never leaving the young writer.

"So nobody would bet on you. I can see that," agreed the

assistant editor. "Your cousin was pretty shrewd to play it that way."

"Yep, he would set it all up; scout the job sites looking for whoever wanted to go for the money; collect bets . . . odds . . . that sort of thing—you know how it works—and the pot would go to the winner . . . and I always got the full pot."

"But, if these ironworkers are as tough as Mr. Mackenzie says they are . . ."

The secretary was completely puzzled.

"I know exactly what you're going to say. 'How could I possibly win?' You know, that was the most interesting part of the whole business. I never had to fight a really good fighter."

"What?" queried the astonished assistant editor. "How did you manage that?"

"Well, for one thing, these fellows—the really good fight-ers—have a code of their own. They're perfectly confident they can take care of themselves when necessary and don't have to prove a thing, so I guess they just couldn't be bothered.

"They knew they could take anybody, and nobody could take them. It was like all this stuff I was getting on with was beneath them. Like it was showing off or something. I think they looked upon my business as a big joke. I remember seeing a couple of them watching one particular fight and they were laughing their heads off."

The assistant editor seemed to understand.

"So, if the really good ones didn't fight, and the run-of-the-mill worker didn't want to—for whatever reason—who would your cousin get for an opponent?"

The writer paused before setting the wineglass down again. When he spoke, he spoke with emphasis, his eyes again resting on the form of the editor-in-chief.

"The bluffs. You know, the guys who thought they were good. The guys who put on this big show of toughness. Going around bullying, shoving people around. Usually people they figured were weaker than they were: what we in Newfoundland call the 'big blows.'"

He was looking directly at the editor-in-chief, but the big man was avoiding his glance. The young writer then resumed his casual tone, glancing alternately to the left and right of his remaining audience.

"My cousin was a genius for sizing up people, and he always managed to find a bluff that lots of people feared but everybody secretly wanted trimmed. . . . That's a Newfoundland word."

He added, almost apologetically.

"They would all show up to watch and bet their money, but when they looked at me you could see their faces drop. Figuring I didn't have the chance of a snowball in hell—and to make sure they didn't lose their money—they felt they had no choice but to bet on the bluff . . . and that's how I made my money."

The editor-in-chief was sitting back, listening intently, alternately salivating and swallowing.

"Now, as everybody knows," the Newfoundlander continued, "guys that bully and bluff are usually useless fighters. That's why they bully and bluff in the first place. Oh, they'd always come out swaggering and crowing, but it wouldn't be too long before they were rolling on the ground, as they say back home, 'not a gig in 'im.' That last guy I pounded must have been in the hospital for five or six weeks. Surgery. . . . Never did walk right after . . ."

He stopped abruptly as the secretary's eyes again opened wide in horror.

"I'm sorry, I got carried away . . ."

The editor-in-chief had begun to perspire profusely as the young writer continued. The latter took another long sip of red wine, holding the glass for just a moment longer to his lips as he again looked straight at the editor-in-chief.

"No, he never did walk again. . . . I was really sorry for what I did to him . . ."

But the editor-in-chief couldn't return the stare. Something was happening that he couldn't explain, that had never happened before. He was experiencing fear—deep, corrosive fear—and he was falling apart. He had caught again the look of hard flint, and he felt the terror course through his veins. He could not fight the panic; he had to leave, he had to extricate himself.

He stood up abruptly, so abruptly that he startled his two co-workers. His voice was hurried in parting, the short, disconnected bursts of speech tumbling upon one another incoherently, making no sense.

"The meeting . . . I had almost forgot. . . . Yes, the meeting. . . . It was moved ahead to seven o'clock. . . . I suddenly remembered. . . . I have to leave immediately . . . already late. . . . Look after this young man here . . ."

In his attempt to free himself from the constraint of the table edge, a cup and saucer smashed on the floor, but he took no notice.

"Mr. Mackenzie . . ." The secretary grasped his arm, trying to restrain him. "The meeting is tomorrow night . . ."

"Yes, yes, tomorrow night. . . . I'll be there . . . yes, yes . . . seven o'clock . . ."

He seemed thoroughly frightened as he stumbled his way through the maze of tables and chairs, now rapidly filling for the evening meal. His secretary tried to call to him over the distance.

"But what about the novel, Mr. MacKenzie? We were going to discuss the novel . . ."

The editor-in-chief half-turned, beads of sweat prominent

on his bulging forehead. He could barely speak above a whisper.

"Discuss the novel? . . . Yes, of course the novel . . . an excellent novel. . . . Yes, we will publish the novel. . . . But the meeting. . . . I can't be late. . . . Yes, yes, publish the novel . . ."

Startled patrons were roughed aside as the editor-in-chief pushed his frantic way through, overcome by panic, driven by some invisible, pursuing force. The assistant editor and the secretary watched as he disappeared past the reception area, totally perplexed by their superior's mystifying behaviour. They had never seen him in such an agitated state.

The young writer's eyes did not follow Mr. MacKenzie's departing form. He seemed to have reverted to his former self: quiet, thoughtful, his sole preoccupation in the moment draining the last of the wine from a nearly empty glass. He then set it down with an air of confidence, simultaneously reaching for the bottle in the centre of the table. As he watched the redness of the liquid slowly rise to the brim, he smiled in the direction of his two companions.

"Well, after all that, Mr. MacKenzie is going to publish my novel. Who would have believed it? He's not such an ogre after all."

His two companions continued to look, stupefied, in the direction their superior had disappeared. The sound of the young writer's voice roused them again to his presence, but they seemed unable to shake the disbelieving looks from their faces.

The secretary was the first to speak.

"My God, I've never seen Mr. MacKenzie so upset."

"No," adjoined the assistant editor, looking directly at the young writer. "Me neither. All that talk you got on with about street-fighting and hospitals and beating up must have really frightened the blazes out of him. You really took him down, and you didn't lift a finger."

The young writer held the full glass of wine at eye level, assuming a mildly dramatic air. He seemed to be examining it before setting it down again. He looked at each of them alternately before replying directly to the assistant editor, a mischievous smile forming on his face.

"Self-defence, my dear fellow . . . the art of self-defence."

THOUGHTS ON RESETTLEMENT

From where I stand I watch the houses slowly
    disappear
Erasing from my memory all those joys of yes-
    teryear
But the world still turns and so I bid my world of
    dreams goodbye
I slowly raise my hand to wipe the teardrop from
    my eye

The towering cliffs are silent in the distance as I
    gaze
They hold my thoughts, my memories, of warm-
    er, softer days
Of people busy making hay, or turning fish to
    dry
Of children gathered on the beach to watch the
    boats go by

The boat reluctant cleaves the send as if it shares
    with me
The feelings that are in my heart, as if it knows
    my misery
I bow my head to hear the restless ocean crash

and heave
And I try to understand the reasons why we have
to leave

They told us that we couldn't stay, the future bids
us on
That we would find our hopes and dreams some
rich place further on
But they didn't tell us how to leave or how we
were to cope
Or how we were to live our lives when we had
lost all hope

With money and fine words they said, they made
it sound so real
But money couldn't pay us for the way it made
us feel
Gone are the days when you would know the
names of all you'd greet
We peer shyly now at faces of the strangers in
the street

The rays of sunlight come to rest upon a little hill
Where those who cannot come with us will be
remaining still
We leave them with their sorrows, and the happiness they knew
Ah, you'd sometimes think they knew no joy, in
the homes in which they grew

Loneliness oft-times held sway, they felt the sea-
sons sting
But they knew joy, and happiness, and they could

dance and sing
And in those houses that now stand abandoned
to decay
The sounds of life were just as rich as any of today

They too could look with loving eyes at a baby
or a bride
They too walked with careless step with a loved
one by their side
And if their laughter was so loud, so wrenching
they could cry
For they also wept, in silent pose, to see their
children die

And so I turn my face and look, to that which
lies ahead
A future that has promised much, but holds its
share of dread
I'll live my life the way I must, but I'll never understand
The way things happened as they did, in those
outports in our land

THE GIRL ON THE VERANDA

I saw her every morning as I stepped onto the veranda to begin my daily journey to the university.

The bungalow where I stayed, like many of the houses on the north side of the Waterford Valley, sat on the slope of a hill, and they were all raised well above street level, having variations of steps and verandas to accommodate the incline of the land. The height provided an excellent view of the valley and the Southside Hills beyond, and I would always stand for a few moments to savour the richness of the morning before descending to the street and beginning my walk to the bus stop.

September is always a beautiful month in Newfoundland, but that year it was exceptional, with clear sunshine and a warm southerly wind every day, and I would pause to absorb the heat of the sun, brilliant on the horizon over the Southside Hills, or to watch the morning mist lie sluggish and heavy in the valley before being dissipated by the advancing heat of the day.

It was one such morning that I first saw her.

The houses were close, almost adjoining, and as I squinted in the direction of the adjacent veranda to avoid the blinding sun, she came within my view. She was sitting in a faded wicker rocking chair, her knees drawn up and her legs bent in the direction of the veranda railing, where her slippered feet rested. This slumping posture caused the chair to tilt backward precariously, but she seemed unaware of the danger of falling.

Her hands held a book which was cradled between her knees, and her body was motionless, except for an occasional movement of her head as she followed the turning of the pages. I did not notice it then, but I remembered after that she did this with a violent hand motion, the harsh slapping of the pages contrasting sharply with the murmuring blend of sounds that made up the autumn morning.

Her long, tangled auburn hair, which she repeatedly swept back with an impatient gesture, kept swirling around her face in the morning breeze. She did not look at me, or give the least indication that she was aware of my presence, or of my immediate and sudden fascination with hers, even as I gazed directly at her. She remained absorbed in the book, oblivious to the fact that she had been the object of my total attention since I first stepped into the morning sunshine.

The appearance of other students hurrying down the street alerted me to the risks of lagging, and I effected a pretend glance at my watch before hastening down the steps to begin my day of classes.

* * * *

I saw her every morning after that.

She was always reading, her slumped posture doing no justice to the youthful shape of her body, which was so apparent the occasional times I saw her stand. At such times she would stretch languidly, or lean over the veranda railing, her arms straight, her hands gripping the railing for support.

These times would last only moments, before she returned in a tired manner to the chair, slumping back into the same unmoving position with which I had become familiar. At times I saw her raise her head to stare intently at the Southside Hills, and I wondered, in my fanciful imagination, if some tragic memory or some deep yearning were the reasons for her gazing with such intensity.

Once, while I was watching some children playing chase in the field across the street, she looked in my direction, but she gave no visible sign that she saw me or wished to attract my attention. She always appeared absorbed within herself, wrapped up in her own thoughts.

She never smiled.

* * * *

None of this, of course, dampened my youthful ardour in the least.

To my adolescent mind, she possessed all that was necessary for an impending friendship. She looked my age, she was pretty, and she lived next door. If anything, her brooding introspection merely deepened the mystery of her personality, sweetened the joy of anticipation.

I was still young and romantic in approach, and surface and appearance were all that mattered. The absence of recognition or conversation on her part never presented itself to me as unusual. I could dismiss it as nothing more than a temporary, fleeting aspect of our beginning together: an obstacle to be overcome in the present, to become a laughable memory in the future, once friendship had taken root, and words and caresses had become ready expressions of uninhibited feeling.

One day, one time, there would happen that chance moment, and there we would be, holding hands, adoring one another in conversation or silence, experiencing the delight of closeness, like all the great literature of love described it. In the meantime, it was only a matter of patience, of dutifully maintaining life's routine until that overpowering moment had arrived, when the metaphoric ice would be broken, and she and I would laugh about those mornings in the past when never a word passed between us.

One could still, like the great lovers of history, admire from a distance, see the sun's rays turn auburn hair to a burnished copper; or linger just one more illicit moment to enjoy the fullness of her tempting body, clad in the loose-fitting white sweater and grey slacks she always wore.

* * * *

I never wondered about the sadness that seemed to be her daily companion, or the shadows that hid her eyes, the rare times they were raised in my direction. I was never curious about her presence every morning on the veranda, or the fact that she was always there before I came out, even when mornings were beginning to take on the sharp chill of the oncoming fall. Neither did I consider it strange that her continuous reading, of book after book, gave her little apparent enjoyment.

I never questioned anything about her.

I was young, I was attracted to her, and that was all that mattered. My most pressing problem was to discover a way to end this daily ritual of observing, passing, and longing, and replace it with one that included walking together, and talking and going to movies at the Paramount Theatre.

It never occurred to me that she wasn't the least bit interested in me. If anything, the unrecognized rejection on her part formed just another part of that mystery surrounding her presence, a mystery which was drawing me inexorably on.

* * * *

The opportunity finally presented itself one afternoon toward the end of September. That morning she had been absent from her usual position in the wicker chair, although the book she was reading lay face down, divided at the spot where she had discontinued reading.

She must have been out before me, but had found some reason to go back in. I had become so used to seeing her the first thing in the morning that I was totally unprepared for the fact that she wasn't there, and I searched for excuses to linger.

I fumbled with my briefcase, lit a cigarette—though I rarely smoked that early in the morning—and even pretended to re-enter the house as if I had forgotten something, to give her time to re-emerge, to see her again as I had seen her every day during September.

I slowly descended the steps one by one, aware that I was running the risk of missing the bus and being late for class, but to no avail. She did not reappear.

Her absence, to my surprise, disturbed me, its unexpectedness contrasting so starkly with the consistency of her daily appearance. It was totally inexplicable, and my youthful imagination gave rein to every conceivable fanciful explanation on the way to the university and throughout the day.

I was distracted for the first time ever during lectures, something my disciplined approach to study would never have permitted up to this point. Her absence that morning was still fresh in my mind as I stepped off the bus on LeMarchant Road and headed down the adjacent street for my return home, filled with dismay that the day had begun so badly.

You can imagine my youthful exhilaration as I turned the corner toward my boarding house to come upon her in full view in the afternoon sunlight. She was not reclining in the wicker chair reading, but was sitting on the steps in front of the veranda, absent-mindedly playing with a long straw of hay which she continually twirled between her fingers, her eyes focussed on the movements of a massive-looking boxer dog that growled menacingly as it played with a discarded tennis ball on the opposite side of the street.

* * * *

My legs slowed, and I felt as if I were pushing my body along. My heart was pounding in my chest, its agitated movement fuelled by the inner excitement which was beginning to surge through me. I would be really close to her for the first time.

I would have to pass directly in front of her, and the long-awaited encounter would happen, regardless of any inhibitions deriving from my want of courage. The anticipated moment had arrived. Common courtesy would dictate that we speak, and the rest would take its course.

In retrospect, I suppose I could have taken an entirely different course and walked on the other side of the street to avoid an encounter with somebody whom I should have known had not the slightest interest in me, but, after all those mornings of maddening speculation, it simply could not go on any longer.

I desperately wanted to meet her.

Besides, the other side of the street was under the unquestionable control of the dog, who had ceased playing with the ball when I came upon the scene, and was eyeing me as if he were hoping I would provoke him into some legitimate retaliation. I instantaneously concluded that whatever the emotional risks of meeting with the unfathomable mistress, they were infinitely inferior to the physical risks of a losing confrontation with her dog.

As I rapidly approached the inevitable encounter, I was by turns apprehensive and resolute. This was the very moment for which I had waited and hoped for three weeks. One smile, one "good day" in the Newfoundland fashion, one meaning-less comment on the weather—under any circumstances an absolute guarantee of conversation in Newfoundland—and it would begin.

The split-second recognition of each other's presence would overcome forever the gulf between us, and bring us both into a whole new world of thoughts and feelings. Whatever happened after that would be, as it says in the marriage cer-emony, in the hands of God. What was imperative now was the beginning. I moved directly in front of her with baited breath. The very next second contained the rise or fall of my emo-tional career.

* * * *

She didn't even look.

I had passed directly in front of her, making it impossible for her to avoid seeing me, and she did not give the slightest indication that I existed. True, her line of vision was broken for an instant, but neither by facial expression or bodily gesture did she acknowledge my presence. She continued twirling the straw of hay between her fingers, staring blankly at no particu-lar point in the distance, her eyes still focused on the dog.

I was dumbfounded.

Not a word had passed between us. We were like two ships passing in the night, unaware of each other's movements, giv-ing no signal, expressing no wonder, uttering no query about the harbour ahead or the storm behind. The meeting on which I had placed such hope and expectation, around which I had woven such dreams and fantasies, had not even taken place.

As I walked away, my feelings of pending excitement changed to feelings of confusion and hurt. I wanted to strike back, to hurt her in return. I wanted to lash out with some sharp, cutting statement, some biting insult, to bring her down from what I perceived to be her distant, lofty, superior perch.

* * * *

Then she spoke. Or rather she called, in a quiet voice that was clear and commanding.

"Come here, Handsome!"

This sudden new turn of circumstance jolted me, exceeding my wildest expectations. I was instantly returned to my earlier feelings. Not only was I being noticed, but noticed for the most singular characteristic which the young male adolescent considers of paramount importance . . . his appearance.

Granted, I had only ever heard it used this way in a jocular fashion, when girls wanted to attract men in a teasing, provocative manner, but I was beyond analysis at that point. She had spoken to me, and that was enough.

I was giddy with joy, delirious with the thoughts of triumph and achievement. That moment, the moment of joyous encounter, the moment which would herald the beginning of a whole new world between us, had finally arrived. But, I could not be compulsive, out of control, immature. She must see me as restrained, with composure.

I had gone the whole gamut of emotions. Moments before I had been excited and expectant, only to be thrust into confusion and despair. Now I had been raised again to the very heights of exhilaration and ecstasy.

I turned to face her, to look for the first time into her eyes, to see unobstructed that paling complexion beneath the flowing auburn hair. I tried to be as nonchalant as I could.

"You called me."

The intent was firm, but my voice was raspy, and I tried

to give my eyes that strong, set look, like the self-confidant heroes in the movies. Her eyes still retained their vagueness, but already that vagueness was slowly giving way to puzzlement as she attempted to grapple with my response. Then her face, which had always looked taut and tense, softened, and a warm smile formed on her lips, the first I had ever seen.

* * * *

She looked at me for what seemed a long time before she spoke, her face betraying uncertainty as to how she should reply in return. When she did, it was in a halting manner, each word gently measured to soften the harsh effect of its content, knowing there was no way to eliminate the devastating impact of her answer.

"I . . . I . . . was just . . ." She stammered, trying to find the right tone for the words. "I . . . was just . . . calling my dog. That's his name."

The last words were blurted out, tumbling over one another, apologetic. Embarrassment overcame me, and I must have been as red as the ore dust we used to see on the Bell Island cars.

But she didn't laugh.

Standing before her was an emotionally helpless, emotionally naked human being, a silly adolescent fool . . . and she didn't laugh. It was in her power to destroy me at that moment, to snicker derisively or lash out with some curt, clipped, demeaning sentence.

She didn't do any of that.

In an instant she had grasped the reality of my situation, the crushing embarrassment of the devastated adolescent; and she didn't laugh. She could not be that cruel.

"What's yours?" she asked quickly. "I'm Mona Collins."

* * * *

For the first time I looked into her eyes, but they were no longer blank and vague. For the first time I saw the real person—the sensitive, compassionate person—behind them.

The sadness had disappeared, the marks of whatever tragedy or painful experience totally dissipated. The soft, understanding eyes, glazed into indifference by too much of whatever her sensitive nature could not withstand, were now beseeching, imploring mine to glimpse the unbelievable coincidence of the events that had taken place; to overcome the feelings of self-hurt and embarrassment, to see beyond the pain of a momentary misunderstanding.

They begged me to see the humour amid the hurt and confusion, to go beyond the trivial and the transitory to the greater richness of life experience; to laugh at the comical, to reserve the times of suffering for real pain.

Then she did laugh. Not in a hurtful way, not in a way that would add misery to my already miserable situation. It was the laughter of healing, the laughter of understanding, the laughter of life.

Her eyes laughed first, and her face glowed, challenging the brightness of the afternoon sun. The laughter infected her whole being, the gentle convulsions of her body creaking the wooden step on which she sat. Even the boxer relaxed his hold on the tennis ball and blinked uncomprehendingly at the sudden change in the atmosphere of the afternoon.

It was not the laughter of contempt or belittlement; it was the laughter of joy, of release, of oneness with the vibrant pulse of life around her. She was hurling defiance at whatever demons of the past or future had been tearing at her soul, her spirits soaring for one brief moment, unconquerable. The rustling of the trees mixed with the sounds of the street to join in chorus, acclaiming in unison with her:

"I cannot be destroyed. I can be free. I am a person."

* * * *

I became aware that I was laughing, too: laughing and transcending. I was laughing with enjoyment, forgetting the misery of silliness I had just experienced, transcending the ridiculous and the superficial.

I had grown a lot in a few minutes.

I had waited so long to know her, but in such a trivial sense. Now I was truly knowing her, knowing her for her compassion, her sensitivity, her understanding. My own emotional clumsiness had placed me totally within her power. With one cold, haughty glance, one sarcastic, cutting remark, she could have destroyed me, defenceless in my immaturity.

Yet in an instant she had chosen to extricate me from a predicament of my own silly making. She must have suffered, or was suffering. All the signs of her exterior person pointed to that. Yet, instead of the retaliation of bitterness, there could still be awakened gentleness, mercy, and humour. In an instant of life she had revealed to me the true nobility of woman.

I would carry that moment with me forever.

* * * *

We parted laughing, and I left the scene to mount the steps to the house, leaving her alone with the gambolling dog. Before I entered, I turned once more to look in her direction. She had not left the steps, still absorbed in the playful activity of the big boxer, but even from that distance I could see her face again assume that cast of sadness with which I had earlier become familiar.

I was perplexed, and I entered the house resolved to dispel the mystery of her mood the very next time I met her, now that the first insurmountable barrier had been hurdled. Perhaps I would engage her from the veranda first thing in the morning, or boldly call on her that evening after supper.

Perhaps I should go directly back and begin where the episode had ended so happily—strike when the iron was hot, as they said. No, I reasoned, time must be allowed to pass to let the full impact of the first meeting take its course.

There would be another day, another afternoon, another meeting.

* * * *

I never saw her again.

I had my first major assignment to do during the night, and I waited impatiently for the morning to come. I hastily gulped my breakfast, to the smiling understanding of my old cousin, and practically ran outdoors, for that first wonderful look, but she was not there.

Again I dawdled.

I set down my briefcase, lit a cigarette, inhaled as I shielded my eyes from the blinding glare of the morning sun, but she did not appear. I could see the dog just beyond the corner of the veranda, but he looked mopish and confused, as if he had lost all interest in life. The tennis ball, with which he had been so engrossed the day before, lay on a storm grate undisturbed.

I picked up my briefcase and walked as slowly as I could down the steps and along the street without appearing to attract attention, keeping my head a little to the side, to catch a glimpse of her out of the corner of my eye, but still her form did not materialize. I did not hear the lectures in class that day, and paid no attention to the debates in the social room.

I was too distracted.

* * * *

That evening I anxiously turned the corner toward my boarding house, as I had done prior to our meeting the day before, full of expectancy for a second wonderful meeting, full of thoughts and plans for another, different conversation, another sharing of a moment, but she was not there.

I kept watching for her day after day, but in vain.

The warm, sunny days of September and early October became bleak and dull as the cold, biting rain of November flooded the streets and howling fall winds stripped the trees of their leaves—and still she did not appear.

The street became progressively more depressing and dismal.

One morning the wicker chair was gone, and I became aware that afternoon that I had not seen the boxer dog in some time. I would still stand on the veranda every morning, even in the cold and the wet and the rain, just for a moment, waiting, hoping for one more chance encounter, but it never happened.

I still walked the length of the street to the bus stop, but I walked more slowly, aware each day that I was walking farther and farther from that beautiful moment of yesterday. On the way back in the evenings I would always look toward the veranda, but my hope of seeing her diminished with each passing day.

* * * *

Snow came early in December, and I went home for Christmas, but it was quiet and uneventful. There were parties and dances everywhere, and lots of pretty Conception Bay girls in flare-tailed dresses and high-heeled shoes, and we played a lot of hockey on Blackduck Pond, but, as the old people say, my heart just wasn't in it.

I kept seeing auburn hair swirling in the autumn breeze, and hearing laughter from a September veranda steps.

I went back to university after Christmas, but things had changed next door. A new Chevrolet was parked by the curb, a lazy Irish setter slept in a makeshift house on the veranda, and two young teenage girls would bolt down the veranda steps every morning on the way to school, always in excited conversation with one another.

* * * *

I had never mentioned any of it to my old cousin, but I was desperate for some information, any information, and I had to approach her with it now. I broached the girl's leaving as disinterestedly as I could to the old woman, for fear of revealing too much of my own emotional involvement, but I need not have worried. Her response was vague, as she shook her head sadly.

"'Twas terrible what was going on there, you know. Such a lovely young girl. Terrible, terrible. He wasn't the real father, you know. Her real father died years ago. Nobody knows where she went . . ."

Then she lapsed into silence. It was the way the people of the older generation had when they simply didn't want to talk about something, when they felt you had to be protected from the harshness of what they had to tell you, when they knew that you were not strong enough to bear what needed to be told. She never told me anything else, and I didn't press her. I finished my meal and went to my room, where I could look through my window at that spot on the veranda.

I cursed myself for being so stupid . . . and so young.

* * * *

A lot of years have passed since then, and some very nice women have been in and out of my life. One has stayed with me and we have lovely children.

I had occasion to drive through that part of town one day last year, and I found myself stopping by my old boarding house and looking at the veranda of the house next door, which really hasn't changed in spite of repairs and new paint and new siding and everything that goes with making an old house modern.

The old couple I stayed with have long since gone to their heavenly reward. Perhaps the girl with the auburn hair who laughed just once is with them.

MRS. MAGINITY'S SLAPPER

Mrs. Maginity's slapper had disappeared. Right out of the classroom, the classroom she had ruled with an iron hand for twenty years.

On a bright, sunny morning in May it disappeared. And not simply disappeared, but stolen. In those days things only "disappeared" when they were taken by the fairies, those little imps of mischief, who were everywhere in the outport Newfoundland world, and who would take things one minute and bring them back the next, just for the fun of it. Like the time Uncle Jim Toomey laid down his splitting knife on the bait bucket and went to reach for it and it was gone. And after he'd cursed and swore and danced a bit right there on the stagehead, he looked and there it was, right where he had left it.

It wasn't like that with the slapper.

The slapper was never seen in Tickles from that day to this, so it must have been stolen. The slapper was on the desk at 11:25 on the thirteenth day of May and was absent at 11:32 on the same day, when Mrs. Maginity went to reach for it to punish big, stund Eddie McClaren for stealing Carrie Ransom's figgy bun, which she still hadn't eaten for recess.

Nobody had actually seen Eddie anywhere near the figgy bun, but since Eddie was the only one who had an established reputation for stealing bread and molasses and raisin buns and anything that sent out a tempting, mouth-watering Newfoundland aroma, he was the most logical suspect. Then where he didn't wash as often as Carrie Ransom liked—being poor and all . . .

However, Mrs. Maginity never got a chance to administer the standard ten on each hand. When she reached for the slapper, it simply wasn't there. Both the bun and the strapper had disappeared, and were never seen since.

And it wasn't the fairies. The fairies always brought things back. And Mrs. Maginity's strapper never came back.

Well, you can imagine the effect this had on Mrs. Maginity. What was she to do now that the very foundation of learning in her school was missing, the keystone upon which the whole edifice of her profession was built? How would the children ever learn to spell words like "ichthyology" and "chthonic"? What reason would they have to memorize those great long answers in their catechism, like "How do you know there is such as state or place as Purgatory," a veritable half-page of daunting perplexity? How would she ever get them to do those great unnecessary columns of arithmetic sums in the back of the book if the slapper wasn't in plain view on the desk, ready to be used as motivation at a moment's notice?

And this was no ordinary slapper.

Certainly not in the same class as those cheap wooden slappers that any Tom, Dick, or Harry—or Jane—of a teacher could procure by lopping off a branch of birch in the nearest grove. This was a strap of the finest leather—a razor strap, in fact—one that had been in the Maginity family for generations, a true family heirloom, having been stolen from a barber in Waterford and brought to Tickles by the first Maginity to come to Newfoundland, where it was used to hone the straight razors of Maginity men preparatory to their daily shaving ordeal.

Of course, the appearance of safety razors on the merchant's shelves in Tickles, and the introduction of the first safety razors into the Maginity household, changed all that, and the old-fashioned razors were put out of business. The razor strap should have been put out of business, too, and consigned to its own honorary nail in the cellar, except that Mildred O'Mullins married Jack Maginity, and became Mildred Maginity, wife of Jack Maginity and co-owner of the razor strap, at a time in her teaching career when her loss of youthful energy and vigour in the classroom were in desperate need of some daily support to prop up her weakening sense of control.

In this way the strap made its transition from home to school, ceasing to become a honer of razors and becoming a slapper of palms, its benefits to the children becoming more and more apparent with each passing day. Even a name change was effected, the instrument in question being referred to now as a "slapper" instead of a "razor strap" in recognition of its more advanced educational role.

In the strong grip of Mrs. Maginity, the slapper became the prime motivator of learning for the thirty-nine students in her charge. This was deplorably necessary, of course, given the fact that many students in those days—including Mrs. Maginity's—had to walk long distances to get to school and would frequently arrive cold and wet—and sometimes hungry—and would need some form of encouragement to learn other than the sole, lonely globe on the table in the corner of the room. Then the intricacies of thirteen times tables had to be mastered, all those names of countries and capitals and the rivers that ran through them had to be learned off . . .

So there it was, prominently displayed on the corner of the desk, as slappers were displayed on school desks throughout the Dominion in those days, easily accessible to be readily brandished, just like the old days of High Noon in the Old West, when to be quick on the draw . . . well, you get the point.

And Mrs. Maginity's slapper was prominently displayed.

Well, it was, until 11:25 on the thirteenth day of May, 1947, and now Mrs. Maginity, you may say, was disarmed, weaponless in the face of thirty-nine students who came to school and sat down and worked and trembled every time she sneezed or coughed. Twenty years of doling out ten or fifteen—sometimes twenty or thirty—on each hand eliminated in one seven-minute period; twenty years of teaching glory consigned to oblivion in the wink of an eye; twenty years of undisputed success in the classroom—there was never a failure in grades nine, ten, or eleven for all that period of time—ended.

Because the slapper was gone.

If education was continue in Tickles it had to be found, and the thief uncovered. If the thief was to be punished for stealing the figgy bun, a heinous enough crime in itself, it had to be found. So Mrs. Maginity set out immediately to find it—at 11:33, to be precise—drawing upon all the tactics she had mastered over the years in the outwitting of students to achieve her objective.

She roved from desk to desk, towering over the smaller students, glaring directly into their panic-stricken faces, loudly demanding what part they played in the slapper's disappearance, but there were no fluttering of eyelids or nervous swallowing or trembling of knees or any such indications of guilt to betray the student criminal.

She assumed a frightening air of the hereafter, appealing to the stern morality of the day, intoning her way sorrowfully through the students like a banker in full sail before an autumn swell.

". . . Even if it's your older brother or sister, you have to tell, because this is a sin against the seventh commandment, meriting eternal damnation in the fires of Hell, . . . even if it's your older brother or sister . . ." she thundered.

But family ties were stronger even than the threatened torments of the eternal underworld, and she achieved nothing. Nobody came forward to claim their reward.

She gave out little slips of paper and ordered the students to write "yes" or "no"—to indicate their respective innocence or guilt—but when the slips of paper were collected, shrewdly matched to the order of the seating plan in the classroom, there was not one "yes" to draw down the fury of her anger or ease her anxious mind.

She would have deprived the entire class of recess and forbidden them to eat their molasses bread and cocomalt, except that the last time she exercised her authority in this extreme manner the entire coterie of mothers from Tickles descended upon the school like a horde of cannibalistic aliens, and she was only saved from a modern-day shredding by the timely intervention of Fr. O'Brien, the congenial parish priest.

Undaunted, she assigned work and sent for the outport constable, who happened to be in Tickles that very morning investigating a similar case of theft, the disappearance of some lobsters from Harry Grogan's lobster pots. The outport constable hurried to the school as fast as he could, fully aware that tardiness on his part in not finding the strap could mean the imminent collapse of the educational system as he knew it. Then with CHE exams just around the corner . . .

He railed as he walked, threatening Salmonier Line and Her Majesty's Penitentiary with a gusto that belied his years, but to no avail. He even produced a pair of rusty handcuffs, which he dangled menacingly in front of little Jimmy Carey's horror-stricken face.

Jimmy Carey, a nervous boy by nature and convulsed into

terror at the thought of spending the rest of his life in the old abandoned jail room under the parish hall, even though he was the last person you'd suspect of stealing anything, howled hysterically in response. The boys in the back couldn't suppress their titters, Mrs. Maginity had to intervene to restore respect for that bastion of Newfoundland outport law, and Const. McMurtle was forced to make a rather humbling exit, muttering something about bringing back the gallows to the head of the harbour and hanging everyone in the class over ten years old.

Since the outport constable did not effect the immediate solution of the crime, Mrs. Maginity then sent for Fr. O'Brien, who, when informed by an excited Carrie Ransom that Mrs. Maginity wanted him "right away," immediately tautened. He was not a man for physical confrontation, and the thought of breaking up yet another fight between the boys from the Cove and the boys from the Point unnerved him to no end. He relaxed, however, upon being informed of the true nature of the request, secretly delighted that the source of so many complaints against the school was so unexpectedly and providentially removed. He was becoming roundly tired of the constant trade of mothers to his back door complaining about the reddened hands of their children.

Still, congenial though he was, Fr. O'Brien was still aware that the authority of his position demanded that he enter the classroom with as much aura of the Almighty surrounding him as possible, especially where it was Mrs. Maginity's classroom. His presence was certain to frighten the truth out of the criminal or criminals responsible and resolve the disappearance in a speedy and efficient manner.

The best he could muster, however, was a sombre expression, totally out of character, which he attempted to maintain while he made a passionate appeal to the student body for the slapper's return. He made frequent reference to the seventh commandment, feeling somewhat hypocritical that he was using this laudable Christian injunction to condemn an action for which he had been secretly praying since his arrival in Tickles.

Fr. O'Brien delivered as good a performance as the authority and holiness of his position—and the presence of Mrs. Maginity—would allow. However, except for Charlie Druken becoming totally overcome by guilt and confessing to having eaten all of the nun's homemade fudge that previous fall when he was in Tarry Harbour—it was left out on the convent step to cool before the school concert—nothing of a significant nature was achieved.

This time the boys in the back burst out laughing, and Mrs. Maginity, chagrined at this display of misbehaviour in front of the priest, launched into her own tirade on obedience to the seventh commandment, ending with a very loud quotation from the old catechism, that those who steal have to return the stolen goods "as soon as possible and as far as they are able, otherwise the sin will not be forgiven them."

Fr. O'Brien, being the newer breed of priest, took advantage of this diversion to glance hurriedly at his watch while murmuring something about an immediate "sick call" in Rancid Bight, wanting at that point to exit the classroom as quickly as possible and escape the wrath of Mrs. Maginity's aging theology.

However, Mrs. Maginity, in an absolute state of shock that summoning the authority of the Church had not been as effective as she had hoped in the recovery of her slapper, had placed her towering frame firmly between Fr. O'Brien and the door, in effect blocking the priest's escape.

"Father, we have to find the slapper. How will the children study? What reason will they have to do their homework?"

Not wanting to be trapped and coerced into another, perhaps more passionate appeal to the students, Fr. O'Brien chose to be consoling, though the attempt at consolation, at least to some of the older students, seemed a trifle shallow.

"You'll find your strap, Mrs. Maginity. I know you will. Say a prayer to good St. Anthony and he'll find it for you."

With this age-old advice, Fr. O'Brien took steps to bring his role in the investigation to a close, taking advantage of his priestly authority to ease around Mrs. Maginity and escape to the safety of his car. Once inside, he glanced toward the back seat to make sure he had his new mail-order fishing rod, then headed in the direction of the Gullies, inwardly thankful that his vow of celibacy protected him from falling into the hands of the Mrs. Maginitys of this world, and hoping that his new fishing rod would be more successful this time against the evasive tactics of the trout of Powery's Pond.

Mrs. Maginity sat behind her desk, eying the students, more exasperated than ever, in a state of total dejection that not even the intervention of the parish priest had brought her one inch closer to the recovery of her beloved slapper. Then, if it were not found, how was she to replace it? Such a valuable heirloom, such an indispensable addition to the classroom.

She thought of paying a visit to the blacksmith in the hill—there were always nice broad bits of discarded horse's harness lying about Dick Cronin's forge—but the memory of Tommy Cronin wringing his hands in pain immediately put that thought out of her mind.

Tommy winced for a week from the thirty on each hand that she had ladled out for his accidentally spilling his ink bottle over his exercise book, and Dick Cronin, respectful and supportive though he was of schools and education in the parish generally, had let it be known to all and sundry that he would brand her with a red-hot horseshoe if she came anywhere near his presence, in retaliation for what he considered an unde-served and unnecessary drubbing. I mean, two or three slaps on each hand for anything was fine . . .

So the thought of visiting the forge was pushed from her mind, as was the thought of borrowing Missy Brown's slapper in the next room—Missy probably couldn't find her slapper, anyway, because she never used it. She was one of those young, silly teachers who thought learning should be enjoyable. And Mrs. Maginity didn't have the legs anymore for traipsing through the woods looking for birch limbs.

And so, in some sense, the search for the slapper ended that day. Though she mulled over the loss of the slapper in the weeks that followed, she couldn't think of any new way to approach her problem, and the disappearance of the slapper became another one of those mysteries for which the outport of Tickles is famous.

Life, inside and outside the classroom, went on, as it tends to do. The warm days of May slowly merged into the warmer days of June, the children bent over their desks scribbling and studying as they had always done, until the final exams put an end to the school year, and the demands and excitement of summer holidays put a temporary end to any thought of the slapper.

However, if the actual search for the slapper was over, discussion about its disappearance was not, especially among the adults of the community, who, as a general rule, are more prone to become concerned about such weighty matters than the children. It was the topic of conversation around the card tables in the parish hall and on the church steps after Mass on Sunday mornings and on the public wharf in the evenings after supper, with first one and then the other offering expla-nation and counter-explanation as to the slapper's strange and mysterious disappearance.

Tom Wilson swore he smelled leather burning when they had the big bonfire on the beach in June, but of course it was impossible at that point to ascertain whether the source of the smell emanating from the fire was the slapper or not. Jonathan Kelly was sure he saw a slapper floating out the harbour in a southerly wind, and a boat was launched, but the "slapper" turned out to be a strip of hide from a poached moose that had strayed into Jim Finnegan's garden. Aunt Jane Wilkins was convinced it was the fairies, but, as I have said, where the fairies always—and dutifully—returned things to their respective owners, after allowing the appropriate time for cursing and swearing and dancing on the stagehead, that explanation was held by fewer and fewer people as time went on.

No, the slapper was never found.

Despite its absence, however, when the CHE results came out in August, everybody had passed, even big, stund Eddie McClaren—after his third year in grade nine. The students soon found themselves into a new school year, and except for the grade elevens moving on and new grade nines coming in, not much changed in Mrs. Maginity's room.

Except that there seemed to be a strange aura of peace in the classroom, as if the slapper weren't needed. The younger children, of course, never really needed such external motivation, and the bigger ones were so busy diagramming sentences and reading *Julius Caesar* for the fifth time that they had all the motivation they could handle.

The aura of tranquility seemed to settle particularly around the gigantic frame of Eddie McClaren, who, in Mrs. Maginity's mind, was the stundest person in the room, and should never have been allowed to pass grade nine in the first place, even after his third year.

No, the slapper was never found.

And, naturally, there were those who blamed St. Anthony

for not coming to Mrs. Maginity's rescue. If so, it was certainly one of the few times St. Anthony failed to respond to a request. But then maybe Mrs. Maginity forgot to ask him, where she was so distraught, or maybe St. Anthony was given twenty or thirty on each hand as a boy in school and was still wincing himself, or being the only spiritual Lost and Found of the day, and stormed by prayers like he was from both sides of the Atlantic, it is possible that he was simply overworked.

No, the slapper was never found, and, as time went on, it became less and less a topic of discussion in the outport, becoming overshadowed, in the days that passed, by another mystery which couldn't be solved either—where big, stund Eddie McClaren, being poor and all, got the nice new soles on his shoes, or "taps," as they called them in those days.

People thought first that the McClarens must have gotten a "barrel" from the 'States, that one of Eddie's better-off cousins in Boston or New York must have sent him a cast-off pair, but closer examination by the more observant in the outport, however, determined that they were not "new" shoes, relatively speaking.

Any fool at all could see that the leather of the upper part of the shoe was black and faded and worn to destitution, while the sole was made of a very find brown leather—a really fancy exquisite leather—not at all like the leather in Dick Cronin's forge. And anyway, when the station master in Flowery heard about it, he was very clear that "No barrel had come from the 'States or from anywhere else for that matter," which put that theory to rest once and for all.

It was strange, too, how the newly soled shoes seemed to blend with the aura of the classroom when Eddie McClaren returned to school in the fall to begin grade ten, which he did for four more years. And it was stranger how the newly soled shoes never squeaked in the presence of Mrs. Maginity, where the leather was so stiff and all. Eddie's shoes did squeak when he was walking up the church aisle on Sunday mornings and when he was walking across the floor of the parish hall when there were dances. In fact, every other place that Eddie walked the soles of his shoes squeaked, but no, never around Mrs. Maginity, as if they were in awe of her presence.

From that day till this, not a shred of evidence was uncovered as to the whereabouts of the slapper. Carrie Ransom went on to become a clerk at Woolworth's. Mrs. Maginity retired when they brought in the new maths. It broke her heart to have to take the old arithmetic book off the desk, and Dick Cronin's forge became a modern-day heritage site, complete with all those bits of discarded harness and the many horse droppings of earlier years.

And big, stund Eddie McClaren?

Well, after he left school, he had a stint down on one of those northern American bases—Crystal I or Crystal II, I forget which—where he stayed three or four years and saved every cent. When he came home he had a bundle. He must have had, because he bought up a whole bunch of those old run-down houses in St. John's and fixed them up and rented them, and now they say he's rolling in money.

He bought a nice house for himself, too, one of those fancy ones there on Waterford Bridge Road. The last time I visited him he was sitting in a little room he called his "den," sipping brandy and eating expensive chocolates like they were going out of style. I happened to notice the old shoes with the fancy leather soles, set on a little table by the old-fashioned Victoria stove.

As I stared at the shoes, I found myself saying:

"They never did find Mrs. Maginity's slapper, did they?"

He didn't reply for a while. He was gazing at the shoes himself. They probably reminded him of the days when he didn't have very much. When he turned to look at me, for the first time I detected a hint, but only a hint, of mischief in his voice.

"Yes, it's a mystery, en't it?"

Oh, by the way, did I tell you that Carrie Ransom and Eddie McClaren got married? Eddie still doesn't wash as often as Carrie likes, but where he's rich and all . . .

MEN OF STEEL

There's a race of men, mighty men, who walk the
    beams on high
And strive with fearless heart and foot to touch
    the endless sky
They carry iron in their grip, these iron men of
    steel
One wonders what they think up there, one
    wonders what they feel

A hundred years ago they left their homes
    around the bay
For cities of magnificence, for all those places
    termed "away"
They left behind each fishing boat, each gaff and
    fishing reel
And put aside ship's rigging to climb girders
    made of steel

New York, Boston, Philadelphia, the names re-
    sound with charm
But that exciting way of living carried danger,
    hidden harm
For harm could come, and come it did, and these

iron men could cry
A thoughtless step, a fateful slip, they watch him
fall and die

So many tales are told of those who died each in
his way
A faulty crane, a collapsed wall, or being simply
tired that day
They walk the walk, they say the prayers, they
comfort those bereaved
Then set their will to climb again, as if they've
never grieved

Yes, go back up again they will, to even greater
height
You'd think that they'd be beaten now, trembling
with fright
But no, and why, and how they do, it's impossible
to say
They'll pause and shrug and tell you that there is
no better way

No better way than span a bridge or a towering
building raise
To watch a hundred storeys grow, that in itself
is praise
Another built, another done, and they can leave
again
And that solid hundred storeys marks the place
where they have been

But when those hundred storeys that they helped
build with pride

Are rent and torn by a terror hand, toppling
  downward side by side
They watch with sadness, grief, and anger as with
  their memories they trace
Every bolt and beam and splice plate that they
  helped put in place

Far out on the ocean floor, above the ocean sands
A tribute to these men of steel, a massive oil rig
  stands
Or mighty dams hold back the force of rivers
  crushing flow
Erected by the skill of men whose names we'll
  never know

They've left their mark on every shore, every city,
  every town
These iron men, these men of steel, these men of
  such renown
Yes, since they first set out to climb, a century has
  spanned
And they've built the whole world over, these
  iron men from Newfoundland

ME AND SAM

Sam had mackerel!

Eight beautiful fat mackerel, with "symmetrical sides and paired organs," just like the student described them to Mr. Agassiz in the literature book that we used in the '50s.

Not being in the mood for the niceties of science while standing on a desolate, windswept harbour wharf at five o'clock in the morning, I could have used more unprintable descriptive words. I was standing beside Sam, my stomach heaving and surging in unison with the waves that rolled past, shivering to death in damp, cold, miserable, Newfoundland fog.

I should have been in bed sensibly snoring under cozy flannelette blankets like everybody else in the harbour. Instead I was heading out fishing on the most dismal morning you could ever imagine to throw out a fishing line along the Newfoundland coast.

And what a morning!

You couldn't see a headland with the drizzle and fog that drenched the far side of the harbour, totally obliterating the hills and coves with its grey, sodden, impenetrable cover.

The icy dampness clung to the oil clothes and cut right through to the skin, making me twitch and shiver inside the uncountable layers of thermal underwear and shirts and socks and sweaters that were supposed to keep me warm.

Strong southerly winds whipped sheets of spray across the harbour over waves that made my stomach queasy. And I wasn't even in the boat yet! Even the little green punt rocking at its moorings seemed to sigh at the unnatural presence of the two grown men standing on the wharf in the early morning darkness in such miserable weather, laden down with fishing gear.

* * * *

Not that I disliked fishing.

On the contrary! I loved fishing. Fishing has always been for me the quintessential Newfoundland pastime. I would look forward with poetic anticipation to those beautiful Saturday mornings in September when the little green punt would plow happily over the friendly waves, surrounded by all kinds of boats and fishermen.

It was a true outport excursion, with bantering and friendly conversation, and fishermen shouting boisterous remarks across the quiet, spacious ocean.

You could inhale the sweet salt air, enjoy the dazzling reflection of the early morning autumn sun on the surface of the gently rocking water. You could take along a drink of hot, sugared brandy, have a mug-up with raisin buns on the afterthwart, and shout jokes across to your friends and neighbours who were always catching more fish than you.

It isn't true what they say about me. I could fish alongside the best of them—when it was calm. Fishing on a beautiful Saturday morning in the midst of a comradely crowd has romance, camaraderie, the aura of good fortune.

But Monday morning! After a late-night dance the night before in the parish hall! In wind and drizzle and fog! The only boat on the water! Waves up to your . . . !

* * * *

Now you may ask, and rightly so, why I hadn't been sensible and gone to bed early the night before, knowing I was going to have, as my stepfather used to say, an early rise.

I reply that I had given the thought careful consideration before going to the dance and had decided that I would leave the dance early and get the necessary sleep, and, in that respect, I was displaying exquisite good sense.

Unfortunately, exquisite good sense, as a general rule, is usually not found in the heads of very young men. A man only acquires exquisite good sense at a later age in life; after he has put untold years of living and hardship and experience behind him; after he has been buffeted incessantly by fate and fortune and acquired that sterling character which only maturity and long life can bring.

Usually twenty minutes after he's dead.

Besides, the band was playing one lancers after another, there were all those pretty Conception Bay girls to dance with, and I had to wait until the dance was over to get the last dance with Matilda Brown to walk her home.

The logic became increasingly clear as the night progressed. It's Sunday night, right! The forecast calls for bad weather on Monday, right! And nobody goes out fishing Monday mornings anyway, right!

So I staggered home at two o'clock, totally exhausted, just two hours before I was supposed to get up and head for the grounds.

Sensible, right!

* * * *

So here we were, Monday morning, five o'clock, bracing ourselves against drizzle-laden gusts of wind on a darkened wharf—me, Sam, and the mackerel.

The mackerel rested solemnly and protectively in a pail between us, their sad eyes bespeaking total lack of awareness of the almost sacred intent to which they would soon be put; one of the last few chances for Sam to stock up on that rare Newfoundland winter delicacy—fish that he would catch and salt and dry cure himself.

Nice, white, bleached, sun-dried cod; salted, washed, and cured to perfection on a flake of spruce boughs, like my step-father, God rest his soul, used to do. Well-watered and boiled, with a dab of butter and a slice of raisin bread—"like angels dancin' over the tip of yer tongue . . ."

For Sam, the mackerel were the road to this delicacy, the passport to plenty, the means to harvest the finny gold of the ocean, the incomparable last chance for winter fish.

To me, at five o'clock in the morning, my eyes burning with lack of sleep, they were eight dead fish that could be turned to better use as fertilizer in some abandoned turnip drill.

* * * *

Sam had mackerel, because there was no other bait to get. Not that this slur diminishes the value of the mackerel one little bit. Mackerel is the best kind of bait. Ask any thinking fisherman—or any thinking codfish, for that matter.

In the hierarchy of baits it ranks a supreme third, after the pre-eminent squid and the succulent clam.

Everybody knows that squid is the absolutely best bait, the *crème de la crème* of baits, the pièce de résistance of culinary attraction in those murky depths of the watery underworld.

No codfish, thinking or unthinking, can resist the tempting allure of a juicy cut of squid, arranged attractively on the hidden barb of a fish hook wafting gently toward the bottom, its black ink trailing seductively back to the surface.

(They're even better stir-fried in a Japanese recipe, but I'm shivering on a wharf at five o'clock in the morning, and if I think too long about warm oriental food I'm going to leave the wharf and go back home and you won't hear the rest of the story.)

Unfortunately, there wasn't a squid to be had in the harbour that year, or anywhere else in Conception Bay for that matter, the very home of the squid. In fact, there hadn't been any sign of squid for years.

You couldn't even go to the cold storage for last year's squid.

There were no freshwater clams, either.

* * * *

We had just had the worst rain in living memory, the rivers and marshes resembled the flooding around the Ark, and those nice, quiet, shallow bends in the river where you'd pick your clams were now raging torrents of wickedly surging water.

But we did have mackerel, the third in line of supreme baits, as I have said, and which are equally capable of hoodwinking unsuspecting codfish. They rank below the unchallenged squid and the sneaky clam, but well above herring and capelin, which are unattractive in their dead state, anyway—even to the human eye—and have a tendency to detach from the hook during the descent to the bottom, leaving the codfish staring blankly at a bare hook.

Codfish can be fooled by clams and mackerel, but there's no way they'll go for a bare hook, since codfish are not as stupid as they look, blankly or otherwise.

Sam said we were lucky to have the mackerel. With the year getting on and still not a fish in salt, they could mean a winter's fish for him. I was going to reply that freezing to death and dying of sheer misery on a heaving wharf was not my idea of being lucky, but what could I say?

He had gone to great pains to acquire what was nothing less than prize bait. One of his buddies from the Southern Shore had gone to a lot of trouble to bring him fresh mackerel on the job the Friday before, and he hadn't frozen them, intending for the both of us to go out Saturday morning. However, Saturday had that howling rainstorm I mentioned earlier. In those days you just didn't go fishing on Sunday— and if we didn't go Monday . . .

* * * *

Perhaps you haven't met Sam.

Sam was my neighbour and one of the best representatives of an older generation that knew fishing exactly like the present generation knows computers—inside out. He could forecast the weather with a glance at the sky, position you dead on the marks on the fishing ground, and split fish almost as good as that taxi driver on the Southern Shore.

(Being slow-moving by nature, he wasn't as fast—the taxi driver on the Southern Shore could have one sound bone going up to meet the other one on the way down—but, in the peculiar way Newfoundlanders have of equating talent, Sam was just as *good*.)

He had fished quite a bit when he was younger, both at home and on the Labrador, but had traded the uncertain and low pay of the fishery of his time for the surer money of ironworking and construction. Like a lot of others of his generation, he retained the old-time skills and still used them every fall to catch a winter's fish, and he could teach you how to cut and split and salt without talking a whole lot about it.

* * * *

So here we were, Sam and I, standing together on the wharf; he, normally quiet and slow-moving, now trembling with eagerness for the quarry, impatient to get a line in the water; me wishing I was anywhere else but next to churning waves that chopped and slapped fifteen tethered boats, raising them and lowering them, raising them and lowering them, raising them and lowering them . . .

I didn't as a rule get seasick, but wave action like that, when you're dead tired and beat to a frazzle, have a mysterious way of interfering with the normal and predictable operation of the human constitution.

So why was I going?

Because I was part of a traditional Newfoundland bargain. I wanted a winter's fish, too. I had the boat and motor—a little green punt with a five-horsepower Johnson motor—and Sam knew how to fish. It was as simple as that. It wasn't all generosity on my part. Without a boat Sam couldn't get to the grounds, and without Sam I couldn't find a fish if I did get to the grounds, with or without the boat.

Since my stepfather died, God rest his soul, Sam was my new partner.

It was a good Newfoundland bargain, but it had a downside. If I didn't go fishing with him when he wanted to—and this morning he desperately wanted to—I could lose my partner, and my chance at a winter's fish.

Standing on the edge of a heaving wharf at five o'clock in the morning dying with the sleep is the downside of a good Newfoundland bargain.

* * * *

We hauled in the punt, climbed down and stowed our gear, and set about leaving. Sam hauled the anchor, coiling the rhode carefully with one hand as he weighed the anchor with the other, while I deliberated with the motor, praying fervently that it wouldn't start.

It worked like a charm.

I swung the nose of the little punt around the array of boats bobbing in unison behind the wharf—should I say giggling in unison—and headed on our outward journey. Away from the protection of the wharf and the breakwater which sheltered it on the lee side, in the open water of the harbour, the little boat began to pitch and roll, not knowing which end was up.

Sam wasn't paying the least bit of attention to me.

To ensure less waste of time on the fishing ground, he had already begun removing the mackerel from the plastic pail and was methodically cutting them into thin slices, big enough to fit over a hook, and carefully laying them for easy access over an improvised bait board that extended across two thwarts.

* * * *

We couldn't talk over the roar of the motor, so we settled down, manner of speaking, to cover the distance straight out the harbour, which I wanted to do as fast as I could; my theory being that the faster we got out there, the faster we could try for a fish and the faster we could get back in—assuming that the fish would be just as appalled at being below the water on such a day as I was at being on top of it. Hopefully they had simply stayed home, or been in schools or whatever.

117

I picked a point on the horizon a little to the right of Salmon Cove Point—I never did learn the difference between port and starboard—and tried to keep the boat reasonably on course in spite of waves that seemed to be bearing down on the aft quarter with more than poetic intent.

"Where are we going?" I shouted over the noise of the motor.

"To the Rock," Sam shouted back, waving his arm in the direction of the mark by that name.

* * * *

The Rock!

I could only think a panicked reply.

Good Lord! Not the Rock. What was he trying to do to me?

I thought he might be deterred by the rough conditions to settle for the calmer safety of Freshwater Cove. You could spit to the shore from a boat anywhere in Freshwater Cove and still catch the best kind of fish. I always caught fish in Freshwater Cove, the biggest kind of fish.

In the tranquility of Freshwater Cove one is perfectly safe. If a boat should sink or be exposed to an unexpected attack from some sea denizen like, say, an eighty-foot-long giant squid or one of those big black-and-white killer whales, you could practically walk to shore in the six shallow fathoms of water.

"Shouldn't we try Freshwater Cove first?"

It was the desperate plea of a desperate man. Perhaps the giant squid or the big black-and-white whales had forced massive schools of huge codfish into the harbour and trapped them in Freshwater Cove just for my convenience.

The Bible is full of ocean-going miracles.

Sam didn't even dignify the question with a verbal response. He just looked toward the cove, his face displaying that peculiar seaman's expression that signifies absolute contempt for anything less than three hundred fathoms of water.

He was still looking toward the Rock.

* * * *

The Rock!

I should have known.

That meant we would be going way outside the harbour—way, way outside the harbour—way, way, way outside until the long, imaginary lines that started from the two churches way back in Harbour Main and Conception Harbour intersected after running endlessly across the roiling expanse of two huge harbours—in the middle of nowhere; an imaginary, obscure spot in the immense, frightening expanse of Conception Bay, where there might be giant squid, or big black-and-white killer whales . . .

I'd seen all the "marks" on a map once, on a nautical map that my brother had spread over the kitchen table. The Rock was just that, an innocuous-looking tip of rock that rose from the depths of Conception Bay and stopped eight fathoms from the surface, removed just a little from the main ledge that ran out from Salmon Cove Point.

The ocean is so beautiful when you're studying it from the warmth and safety of a modern kitchen table.

From the vantage point of the lowest end of a small green punt in the middle of churning water it looks downright murderous. All I could see was angry, furling water, foam-topped, in constant motion, curling endlessly toward the grey, heaving horizon.

* * * *

We passed Moore's Head and Shipcove Rock and soon the houses of Gallows Cove were behind us. I closed my eyes and sucked in my breath as we rounded Gallows Cove Head and a big cross wave struck the punt, lifting her sideways.

The head was still a mile away—in outport terms—but I had visions of climbing it, soaking wet, from the ocean side. Sam, seemingly glued to the thwart of the fore-standing room, swayed with the motion, patiently attempting to affix a piece of mackerel to one of the hooks on his fishing line.

There's no sense in not being ready.

We inched our way through Freshwater Cove, past the Straight Cliff and into Ram's Horn Bight. The wind picked up, and I wondered about the necessity of going all the way to the Rock when we were doubtless passing uncountable fish directly beneath our feet, or our bottom, as the case might be.

It wouldn't hurt to try again.

"Sure you don't want to try in Freshwater Cove?"

Sam was swishing the knife blade in the water to clean it. He turned and looked over the Cove again, as if weighing my request, the knife blade still trailing in the water. The motion gave my spirits hope. I had always known him to be a sensible man.

"Nothin' in Freshwater Cove. Not like there used to be."

He spoke with a surety of knowledge, with a finality of tone. He could not have seen the sinking feeling on my face.

"We'll try the Rock first."

There would be no further discussion.

* * * *

It had gotten rougher as we plowed across Ram's Horn Bight, but it was nothing compared to the open water of the bay as we passed the lighthouse and struck out toward the

Rock. My mind must have been subconsciously directing my steering arm to hug close to the cliff of Salmon Cove Point, because I became aware of Sam repeatedly swinging his arm outward, a concerned expression on his face.

I wasn't getting off that easily.

The stretch from Salmon Cove Point to the Rock was pure horror, and the waves must have come straight out of a Joseph Conrad novel.

Sam rocked and swayed with the plunging movements of the boat, alternately looking toward the Rock to make sure we were on course, then back to the neatly arranged strips of mackerel on the bait board. You could tell by his eyes what he was thinking.

"If every one of them is a big fish . . ."

* * * *

Somehow we got to the Rock, and Sam threw out the anchor, waiting for it to settle and take hold before paying out some slack and looping it around the stem post with two "half-itches."

Anxiety overpowered me.

Up to that point I had to focus all my concentration and energies on handling the boat in the rough water, to the exclusion of all other damaging thoughts. The constant movement of the boat assured me that at least we were still afloat, that getting there was of prime concern.

It had not occurred to me that, once there, all of my motivation to remain in control would instantly disappear, that I would be anchored, literally, to one tiny pitching spot on the ocean surface, where I was helplessly trapped, indefensible against whatever horrors the raging sea wished to unleash.

As the graplin hooked in the bottom and the boat turned

into the wind, I took in my situation at a glance, and was overcome with abject terror.

From the aft room of the heaving boat I became frighteningly aware of the immense expanse of grey rolling water that separated me from the nearest land, the waves that crested and crashed around the boat, the spume that curled in around the gunnels—and that was just the front.

When I looked around and behind toward Bell Island and the horizon, and the illimitable reaches of Conception Bay, I saw only one outcome of the morning, only one certain possibility—the pair of us drifting endlessly, bottom-up, clinging in desperation to the keel in the freezing water . . .

Sam's line had already hit bottom, and he measured it back an arm and a half's length, holding it looped around his right hand while he steadied himself against the gunnel with the other.

* * * *

I just couldn't stay.

The tautness that had been slowly forming in the depths of my stomach flooded through my body and blurred my mind until I became a numb entity, unable to control the feelings of helplessness and terror that swept over me. The water swirled in front of me, making me dizzy. I expected to faint and pitch right in any second.

"Sam! I can't stay."

That was all I said. He looked at me for just a moment before beginning to haul up his line.

"You're the boss."

He said nothing else. It was an acknowledgement of the fact that I owned the boat, pure and simple. These people didn't waste time, energy, or motion.

If I couldn't stay, there was only one other alternative.

He finished hauling in his line and hauled the anchor over the plunging prow of the boat, planting his feet wide and securing himself with his knees against the cuddy, while I got the motor going and we headed in. Then he sat on the thwart in silence and slowly reeled up his line, setting it carefully back in the bucket of fishing gear in the midship room.

He continued to sit in silence as we headed toward the harbour, his eyes never leaving the rock behind us.

The day had suddenly become even more dismal.

* * * *

We stopped at Freshwater Cove on the way in, and for the third time I prayed earnestly. We moored fairly close to the shore, baited up and threw out the lines, then sat patiently, feeling for the fish in the relative comfort of the sheltered lun. I was reminded of the school poster—"Ships are safe in harbours, but that's not what ships are for."

Everything was perfect as far as I was concerned—except that the fish were somewhere else.

Where were all those fish I used to catch years ago?

I perked up in anticipation as Sam's line suddenly went taut and he rose to a half-crouching position, straining at the line. Thank you, Lord. I leaned over the gunnel breathless with excitement—to watch as a massive flounder churned the water in resistance.

That was a clear message.

If the bottom flounders could get at the bait, there wasn't a codfish within an English mile.

Just as dejection returned, I was heartened by an immense tug on my own line and I could sense Sam look in my direction expectantly. I was not to be rewarded so easily. After straining happily for what seemed like a very long time to haul the resisting weight to the surface, I was appalled to find myself staring sickly into the malevolent eyes of a huge wolfish, glaring at me menacingly over the gunnel of the boat, his orange-edged blackish-grey tail thrashing the water viciously.

You haven't seen evil until you've looked into the eyes of a wolfish over the gunnel of a boat at six o'clock in the morning.

The intent of the look was clear.

"If you don't get this hook out of my mouth right now, I'm coming right in over the gunnel of this boat . . ."

I got the gaff and wrenched the hook free with that practised motion my stepfather had taught me, then slid back along the thwart into the safety of the boat as the wolfish crashed into the water. Before he dived he turned and gave me one last look that said—

"If you ever . . ."

I sat on the thwart and wished for a cigarette, but I had given up smoking five years before, and anyway my hands were soaking wet. I glanced forward in Sam's direction to watch him as he carefully rolled up his line and deposited it carefully a second time into the plastic pail.

That was an even clearer message.

* * * *

Sam hauled the anchor again and the boat drifted back as I repeatedly hauled on the starting cord.

"Want to try somewhere else?"

It was a meaningless question, but I had to say something.

"You're the boss," came the reply.

The tone wasn't as harsh as before, just disappointed. God put a thought in my mind.

"Let's try the Ledge," I shouted over the motor, which had

started just in time to get around another big wave that was bearing down.

You could catch big fish on the Ledge, really big fish, clever fish.

Sam looked at me in disbelief. The Ledge was on the other side of the open harbour mouth. A lot of rough water separated us from the Ledge. He looked across the foam-tipped open expanse we would have to navigate in our small boat and he looked back at me, still in disbelief, before he nodded his head affirmatively.

We would try the Ledge.

Now the reader might be wondering where I got this sudden—and surprising—infusion of physical and psychological courage; why I had fled the Rock in sheer terror literally minutes before but was now embarking on just as deadly a trek across the fully exposed waters of the harbour mouth, to a fishing mark that was just as open and dangerous as the one we had left.

The fears and terrors had disappeared. Perhaps it was the brief respite in the tranquility of Freshwater Cove; or the quiet, calming presence of my companion, dispelling my silly fears. Wherever it came from, the old "narve" had returned. Still a bit queasy, as they would say, but with enough sense to trust the older man sitting on the forward thwart.

If he didn't see any danger, maybe there just wasn't any.

Besides, I was thinking straighter now. As everyone familiar with the Ledge knows, on the new mark Bell Island would be straight behind us. If the punt did flip over and we had to cling to the keel, we would only have to drift eleven or twelve miles before someone would see us and pluck us out.

They're always looking up the Bay from out there . . .

* * * *

The trip across was exactly as I had expected, an eternity of endless waves. I was drowned in the spray that kept crashing over the side of the boat, and had to bail a good bit with one hand as I manoeuvred the boat with the other, but we finally arrived. Sam took a reading on the imaginary lines that positioned us on the mark, carefully directed me left and right, and then dropped the anchor in a spot I was familiar with, from many such experiences with my stepfather.

His choice of a mark on the inside part of the Ledge told me that even he preferred being where we were. I could read from his looking out over the water that the outside ledge would be impossibly rough in a small punt. He was a skilled fisherman, with no fear of the ordinary sea, but even he knew that respect had to balance courage, at least where the sea was concerned. He was no fool, either, as they say.

We baited up and threw down the lines, and I sat back to enjoy the rise and fall of the boat, watching the bait and sud lines quickly disappear from sight on the way to the bottom. I prayed again, only this time it wasn't silly and foolish like before. It was just a brief thought that appeared as I looked out over the never-ending waves while feeling with my line—

"Put some fish under the forward part of the boat, just a few, please."

* * * *

Well, sir, someone must have been listening, because just about then Sam's line tautened like a Mongol bowstring and he half-straightened, straining with all his might against a line that seemed to be hooked in the anchor of a Bell Island ferry.

That meant only one thing, a big fish—a very big fish.

And big it was. He hauled in a fish that would make Guinness proud. And that wasn't the only one. I could see the excitement that couldn't be stilled in the quiet eyes and on the aged demeanour of the windburned face, and I simply felt happy.

The rest is epilogue, as they say. Sam got twenty-four big fish that morning, prompting me to coin a saying that when you pair up persistence with mackerel for bait, even on a rough morning, you're bound to succeed. I haven't seen it on a matchbox cover yet, so I suppose the saying hasn't caught on.

I got five, but as every inshore fisherman knows, the fellow in the forward part of the boat always gets more fish, anyway. Besides, I had prayed for the fish to be forward, not aft, and if your prayers get answered the way you want, you really can't complain.

Time was getting on, we had exhausted the mackerel, and twenty-nine big fish was as good as you could ask for under the circumstances. It would be a fair bit of work for an older man to split and clear away. Sam looked over the water—I had sensed the wind rising myself—and began to leisurely reel in his line.

"'Tis time for us to get in out of this now."

* * * *

I wasn't unhappy with his decision. Sleeping in your own little bed is vastly superior to trying to catch up on sleep in the aft room of a small punt which is attempting calisthenics in an open sea. I rolled up, started the motor, and nudged her into the wind to ease the strain on Sam hauling the anchor.

It seemed like it was going to be a pleasant trip home and I was getting all ready to put that part of my past behind me, when the wind suddenly came out of nowhere to turn the Ledge into something close to a raging maelstrom. The little punt rocked and plowed like a toy sailboat in a bathtub, and for the first time that morning, the thought struck me that we could actually drown.

I had to express my fears to Sam in some way.

"It's getting a bit rough."

In all of that roaring motion with wind and spray drenching the boat, Sam had somehow gotten a cigarette from the package in his pocket into his mouth and was trying to light it with a lighter, using the top flap of his oil pants for a shield. His reply was mildly reprimanding as he blew smoke through the side of his mouth.

"Me and your stepfather rowed in worse mornings than this."

Well, that certainly put drowning in perspective.

* * * *

That was one of the last times I fished with Sam. His legs gave out that following spring—he couldn't climb up and down the wharf—and when I extended my annual invitation the next fall, he declined in the factual way his generation used.

"I'm gettin' too old, now, b'y. 'Tis time for a younger man to take over."

He lived a good few years after, splitting an occasional fish for me, maintaining good health and keeping in touch, watching me over the fence or through his living room window those nights I had to check the boat off the rocks or tighten her up on the frape if the wind came northeast.

He died the way he lived, quietly, without fuss, and with his death the old generation was reduced by yet another incredible human being.

I still maintain my presence on the grounds—well, if you consider Freshwater Cove part of the grounds. I have a somewhat bigger boat now, a yellow one with a heavier motor, and on nice days with lots of boats around, I'll go way out—sometimes way, way out—because if the waves ripple either bit at all, you can put her on full throttle and be in out of there, sir, before a gull swallows a capelin.

Mostly, though, I stay around Freshwater Cove, catching the odd small fish, enjoying the gentle rolling of the punt on the water, trying to hear the gurgle of the little brook that gives the cove its name, marvelling at the monstrous bald head of Gallows Cove Point, the striking geological precision of the Straight Cliff, the majestic sweep of Ram's Horn Bight . . .

It's so beautiful in Freshwater Cove—so perfectly safe; no giant eighty-foot squid, no monstrous black-and-white killer whales . . .

REVENGE OF THE FAIRIES

Abie Dutton didn't believe in fairies. In fact, he didn't believe in anything he couldn't see with his eyes. He didn't believe in dinosaurs, either.

"Just a bunch of big, old sheep bones . . . big, old sheep bones," he would say, in a really irritated tone—and he didn't believe in fairies.

In fact, he scoffed at the whole idea of fairies, and laughed his head off every time somebody else came back talking about being mesmerized in the woods. When Abie heard that Jim Pat O'Donnell had spent the whole night on the other side of the style because the fairies wouldn't let him climb over, Abie's snarky comment was that Jim Pat was always "too bloody lazy to lift his feet, anyway." And when the Muckler lost his splitting knife that time, Abie said something like "G'way, b'y, the Muckler is as forgetful as me old grandmother, anyway . . ." and showed no sympathy for the old man at all.

No matter how late it was at night, after a card game Abie would never turn his coat inside out, and he never carried bread in his pocket or a bit of change no matter where he went in the woods. When the other men, aware of the presence of the little people, would respectfully step over a fairy path or avoid a fairy circle, Abie would simply barge right through whistling. He would even trample down the fairy caps[1] that the wee people used as seats to rest, and not give a care in the world to what he was doing.

This horrified the men who were with him cutting wood or trouting or setting rabbit snares, and they would say things to him like—"Abie, you'd better watch what you're doing" or "The fairies aren't going to put up with that too long, my son . . ." They would shake their heads in consternation and go about what they were doing, knowing that someday Abie was going to get himself into a whole lot of trouble.

When his mother would plead with him to put a crust of bread in his pocket, anxious for his safety, Abie would thrust his arms out into his sleeves and smack his back pocket with a derisive sneer and stride out, leaving his poor mother in a terrible way.

He wasn't even afraid to face Aunt Sarah, who was renowned throughout the Bay for her intimate knowledge of fairies. She had seen them numerous times on her rambles during the nights and had even watched a complete fairy dance one bright moonlit night that previous May.

"Not as all as fast as the lancers here, my dear," she said. "More like one of those slow reels they does in Nova Scotia or Cape Breton. They goes up and down more . . ." She had a deep respect for the fairies, just like the respect you'd have for the reverend mother in the parish convent, which explains why they let her watch their dance and were cordial to her whenever she did meet them.

Abie didn't have that kind of respect. Once when Aunt Sarah tried to give him advice, he behaved terribly altogether.

---

[1] Since the relegation of fairies to folklore, fairy caps have been renamed mushrooms and are used mainly now for eating. See also TOADSTOOLS.

"If you meet a fairy," his Aunt Sarah said, "take three steps backward and turn around three times with your eyes closed. That's a mark of respect for them and they will pass you by and leave you alone."

This, of course, set off Abie in the gales of laughter, and he turned around four or five times right there in front of his Aunt Sarah as a way of flaunting her advice.

"The fairies will take you, my dear, and you'll never come back . . ." his Aunt Sarah said sternly, shaking her head. At which Abie walked off snorting with laughter.

Sister Mary Dismas even took him aside one Sunday morning after Mass (her great-great-grandfather had come straight from Ireland before the famine) and tried her best to warn him of the dire consequences of his unbelief, but to no avail. Abie went on his merry way, saying unkind things about nuns and fairies and Irish great-great-grandfathers who believed such silly stuff.

Now you may suspect that the fairies didn't like this one little bit. It upset them terribly that Abie showed absolutely no respect for their paths and their circles, but it incensed them to no end that he trampled on the fairy caps, the only places in fairyland where they could sit after a long night dancing, and some of the older fairies had made loud protestations to Raguna III, the reigning fairy queen.

They didn't mind people simply not believing. They had kept up on developments in the modern world and understood that when people in the outports got educated and read books and newspapers and procured televisions and street lights and things that they would stop believing in anything they couldn't see, like angels and spirits and ghosts and whatever. So they weren't particularly upset by disbelief. I mean, nobody seemed to be believing in anything anymore. But to be treated with such scorn! Such contempt! As if they had never existed.

No, they didn't mind at all that people didn't "believe." They were happy enough in their own world rolling Jackie Lanterns across the bogs when it got dark, having their wee dances at all hours of the night, sipping honeyed nectar while lazing on their fairy caps, and, of course, playing the odd trick, like leading somebody astray in the woods for a little bit before they put them on the right path and hiding things for a few minutes and stuff like that. But they never took babies. Queen Raguna herself was clear on that in the first ever fairy interview on radio.

"Oh, no," she said. "Never babies. It was terrible how they started that story, you know. In County Cork, I believe it was, in my great-great-great-grandmother's time. They wanted to make us look really bad because they thought we were siding with the authorities in the rebellion, which, horror upon horrors, we weren't. . . . Oh, no, never babies. . . . We'll lead the odd big one astray, just to teach him a lesson about minding where he's going in the woods and such. And we'll take a splitting knife or axe or whatever for a few minutes to make sure people won't be forgetful about laying sharp things like that around where there are small children. . . . But heavens no. Never babies . . . never babies . . ."

And on that point she was very strong.

But, as I say, to be treated with such contempt and scorn. Such ridicule. To be treated as if they didn't even exist. That was unbearable.

So it was widely agreed among the fairies that Abie should be taught a lesson. Since the matter was of such import—punishing a human—only a decision from a full meeting of a council of elders of the whole island could approve such a drastic step, given the ramifications that could ensue if the human world chose to retaliate. So to debate the appropriate course of action, invitations were mailed to seventeen extant fairy circles to send a representative to Goose Marsh Fairy Circle for deliberations—Abie being in their jurisdiction—to be held on the first full moon in August after sunset, weather permitting.[2]

The weather was extremely favourable on the appointed night, a great big round moon beaming down the fullness of its light on the open fairy hills on the souther side of the Goose Marsh, so the representatives of all seventeen fairy circles gathered in a supreme circle on designated fairy caps, with Queen Raguna III occupying the place of honour on a large fairy cap to the north of the circle, as befitted her rank as reigning queen and host of the gathering. A battalion of the Queen's bodyguard, the Royal Elfin Sprites, armed with the new magic wands and looking very smart in newly painted yellow wings and royal purple colours, milled about directing people to their fairy caps and keeping a watchful eye for the appearance of members from the Burin Peninsula circle, in the event that they should crash the meeting.

She very quickly began proceedings.

"Honourable members of the Supreme Council. You all know why you are here. We have been living on favourable terms with the humans in Newfoundland ever since we first arrived here from Waterford, and the humans in turn have given reciprocal respect. Whether it's carrying a crust of bread in the pocket as demanded by Ordinance 745 when proceed-

---

[2] The Burin Peninsula fairy circle was not invited since that debacle over the Supreme Council's decision to ban the changing of animals in stables for fun, a notorious form of mischief that was instituted in County Clare in the early 1800s and was never sanctioned by the great majority of fairies. The Supreme Council felt it imposed too great a hardship on poor families. The Burin Peninsula Circle has refused to this day to honour the ban.

ing past fairy country or turning the topcoat inside out as demanded by subsection 32 of Ordinance 846 when proceeding at night during monthly festivals, humans to date have been diligently and meticulously co-operative. So we are not at war with the human world . . ."

At this point various expressions of affirmation could be heard, such as "Hear, hear . . ." "True, true . . ." and "That's right, that's right . . ." There were shouts, too, of "Don't lose it, maid" and "Heave it outta ya, Raggie . . ." and "Way to go, girl . . ." from younger members who were now developing a new Newfoundland language and who had been imbibing too much fermented nectar.

". . . No, we are not at war with the human world. But . . ." and here she assumed a stern, almost angry tone, ". . . we are at war with Abie Dutton . . ."

Here there was a great thumping of magic wands on tree stumps.

". . . So I ask for suggestions for dealing with what we can only describe as a very obnoxious human being . . ."

Here there ensued a general murmuring and nodding of heads as the gathering attempted to conceive of some plan, a collective sound that abruptly ended when a little, wizened old fairy, Oberjaun by name, strode to the giant fairy cap that served as a podium. All eyes followed his movements because Oberjaun had developed quite a reputation as a wise and knowing fairy. He had already published one book on "Analytic comparisons of diverse Miscellania in Fairyland: Divergent genetic compilations of Irish Fairies" and was highly respected on both sides of the Atlantic for his thorough knowledge of the involvement of Irish Fairies in the Atlantic fish trade of the 1600s. (They were particularly good at moving the schools of fish from one mark to another, to torment fishermen they didn't like. Which explains why one fisherman could be loading the boat while another twenty feet away wouldn't be getting a nibble.)

He mounted the podium with ease and began to address the assembly.

"Fellow fairies. I will be brief. I recommend that I be given authority to lead Abie Dutton astray in the woods and subject him to the Twelfth Compendium of punishment before returning him to the human race."

A collective gasp greeted the request, resounding throughout the assembly. The eighth and tenth compendiums were harsh enough, but to approve the Twelfth Compendium. . . . Well.[3] The last time in living memory that was approved resulted in Sir Humphrey Gilbert being lost at sea and never being heard from again, although there are some fairies to this day who assert that something must have gone wrong with the spell because Sir Humphrey was not supposed to be drowned, only lost for a while.

After some deliberation, the Twelfth Compendium was reluctantly approved and Oberjaun was given the authority to punish Abie Dutton as directed, but not to go beyond that. It was further stipulated that the term of punishment was not to exceed one calendar year from date of implementation. If Abie did not mend his ways by that time, a further meeting would be convened to accept a report and decide if further action was warranted. Some of the older fairies were concerned that the spell might malfunction as they thought it did in the case of Sir Humphrey and that real harm would come to another human, something they could only view with abhorrence.

Since there was no further business, the fairies agreed to

---

[3] Fairies never deal in odd numbers and always count by twos. This is believed to ensure good health and prosperity, and is particularly good for wing strengthening in cold weather.

adjourn the meeting, an adjournment that was duly noted in the minutes. Queen Raguna then formally declared a night of dancing, honeyed nectar was provided in buttercups, and the night ended on a festive note, as is demanded of fairies in Article 3 of the Fourth Covenant. Oberjaun left the dancing early to prepare for his meeting with Abie and to review all the chants necessary for the various punishments he was about to inflict.

What happened after is recorded in the third book of *Assizes of Compendia* and is available to fairies worldwide at the appropriate flick of a wand. It was made available to the author upon provision of thirteen crusts of stale bread deposited on the Second Fairy Hill at dawn on the summer solstice, the twenty-first of June.

Oberjaun accosted Abie in a wood-path the next morning, disguised as a tourist, complete with sunglasses, sandals, Bermuda shorts, and matching shirt. Abie wasn't the least bit intimidated by the sudden appearance of one so short, since Hayward Little and all his cousins in Bunion Cove were just as short as that, and, he thought wickedly "Just as pore-lookin'," noting the fairy's crooked stance and the wizened-looking face. Their conversation was recorded verbatim in Oberjaun's new magic wand, which along with casting spells to make people mesmerized and having things disappear and return, was now equipped with those new chip implants for data retrieval. Oberjaun spoke in the Newfoundland dialect of Notre Dame Bay, with which he was most familiar, and got right to the point.

"How's she goin', Abie Dutton? I'm from Fairyland. And I think it's time for a spell."

"I think I'll take one meself," replies Abie in a jaunty tone, and he rested his axe by a big spruce stump as he sat on a old dry "whiten."

"From Fairyland, eh!" Abie continued, smirking, as he eyed the little creature in front of him. "You must be one of those little fairies I hears people talking about."

"I am that," scowled Oberjaun, "and I'm here to teach you a lesson about fairies."

"Well, have it out of ye," laughs Abie, thinking it was one of the short Mullownys from across the ridge having a game. "I'm all ears, and I don't have that much wood to cut, anyway."

"I'll give ye one last chance, Abie Dutton. Will you change your errant ways and believe in fairies, so that you can give them the respect they deserve?"

(Under the terms of the Twelfth Compendium, this question must first be asked before any further action is taken.)

At which point, of course, Abie doubles up on the stump, and was a good while laughing. Then he grins a wicked grin, his eyes twinkling. You had to give the short Mullownys as good as they sent.

"Sure, if you're a fairy, turn me into a frog or something."

"No, I can't do that," Oberjaun replied seriously. "I'm not allowed. But I have been given authority to cast a spell. So don't say I didn't warn ye."[4]

So saying, Oberjaun mounted a giant fairy cap, danced a number of steps, said something in a very strange Irish dialect while waving his wand in Abie's direction, then bowed solemnly before hopping down from the fairy cap and disappearing. Abie clapped his hands vigorously in applause, then re-

---

[4] There is some suggestion that the first spell didn't work, that Oberjaun slipped while waving the wand. The spell missed Abie and hit a black bear standing by the river, turning him into a coyote, suggesting that coyotes didn't come from Quebec over the ice after all.

verted back to doubling over with laughter, his usual response to anything remotely related to fairies.

He was still laughing as he went to lift his axe to be on his way. But the axe wouldn't budge, and when Abie peered close, it was actually frozen to the ground.

"But it's August," Abie thought. "How can it be frozen . . . ?"

So he grabbed the axe by the haft, and after three or four big yanks, it came free, because of course, fairy tricks are only temporary, and are only meant to torment and irritate, and are not meant to have any kind of permanent result.

Then when he went to cut down a tree, a great big birch, the axe wouldn't cut. No matter how hard he swung, or how deep he took a breath, or how strong he gripped the haft, the blade just touched the tree and barely scratched the bark.

"I'm tired," said Abie. "That's what it is. I shouldn't have done all those lancers last night at the dance, not getting to bed until four o'clock . . ." And he thought no more about it and went to gather up some old dry branches to take home for firewood. But the branches seemed to have taken root in the ground again, and it was only by tugging with all his might that he could get one free, and he was pretty beat out by the time he got home.

And that's how it went for Abie as the fairy spell settled over him day by day. He went picking blueberries, and every single berry turned white before his eyes, and he returned home without a single berry in his pail. He went squidding in the punt with his Uncle Martin, and every single squid he caught squirted down his throat, just like in the song, and he had to give up and go ashore, much to the disgust of his Uncle Martin, because squids were fifty cents a hundred and Uncle Martin was planning on loading the boat with his new big dip net.

Day in and day out, as the year went by, no matter what he turned his hand to do, Abie was haunted by the spell. In

October he ran out a few lines of trawl, but every time he hauled there was nothing but sculpins on the hooks, and he left the trawl in the water and tied up the boat to the wharf. At the first Christmas party in Uncle Jim Casey's kitchen, he took up the accordion to play a tune, and the yard filled up with moose and caribou bellowing and stomping, and they had to ask him to stop while they drove all the animals away.

He had to give up playing hockey on Waver's Pond because every time he shot the puck at the other goal, the puck would curve away and miss, bounce off a rock on the side of the pond, and shoot past him on the way back to go in his own goal, and his team would lose by a big score every time. When the spring came and he had to fence the pasture, the harder he hit the stakes, the more they came up out of the ground.

It was only after he began to see really strange things at night that Abie began to realize that he was in trouble, that maybe the fairies had something to do with it after all. Coming home from the kitchen racket at Aunt Rosie Clanning's at three o'clock in the morning, the pile of lobster pots by Hap Reardon's stage turned into a killer whale that began to follow him home, walking on six big legs. A bunch of maiden rays flying over the wharf called to him, asking him if he enjoyed the time at Aunt Rosie's, and a whole slew of big harbour seals, each with his own fiddle, were playing 'er up on the head of the wharf, while a whole bunch of fish danced and swung their partners.

That's when he panicked. The sweat was pouring off him as he ran home to wake his mother, who of course knew from the beginning what was going on, and immediately sent him to wake his Aunt Sarah, who would tell him what to do.

Aunt Sarah, dressed in her nightgown with her rollers in her hair, wasted no time in admonishing him.

"I told you, my dear, I told you . . ." she said, shaking her head sorrowfully. "Now what you have to do is go back to that same spot, while it's still dark, sit on the same 'whiten' with your axe laid down exactly as it was the day you met the fairy. You bow your head, close your eyes, and say as loud as you can, 'I believes in fairies, I believes in fairies . . .' ten times, right slow. The fairies will hear you, because this time of night they're walking their circles, and they will come and lift the spell."

Well, that was all Abie needed to hear.

He grabbed his axe and walked as fast as he could to the grove where he had first seen Oberjaun, followed by the killer whale on his six big legs and the flying maiden rays. He laid his axe by the same spruce stump, then sat on the same "whiten" exactly as Aunt Sarah had commanded. Closing his eyes really tight, he began "I believes in fairies" in a very contrite tone.

Of course the fairies had been watching him come, and were so glad to see a human, especially a human like Abie, to be so repentant, that they converged from all parts of the island in a circle around him, with Queen Raguna again occupying the place of honour on a huge fairy cap to his right. When Abie had finished the tenth "I believes in fairies," she directed Oberjaun to assume a commanding position on the foremost fairy cap and lift the spell, which he did very quickly with a short incantation and only two waves of the magic wand, which of course is all that is necessary when a human is truly repentant.

Just like that the spell was lifted, the whale and the maiden rays disappeared, and Abie felt very relieved. He shook hands with Oberjaun and some closer fairies, bowed respectfully to Queen Raguna, picked up his axe, and headed home, whistling happily all the way.

And how did things work out after, now that the fairies were his friends? Well, my son. The next year he filled the boat with squids every trip, caught the biggest kind of fish on his trawl, and played that accordion so good everybody in the outport shook their heads in wonder. And as for the hockey the next winter, he scored that many goals on the pond that a scout came down from one of them big teams in Canada and brought him up to Toronto somewhere and he got on a fourth string and saw every game they played that year from the box.

So. Did Abie believe in fairies after that? Well, I suppose he did.

A SOCIAL VISIT

The car I had at the time was a little blue Viva, which, as those with the least inkling of interest in automobile history would know, was a very, very small car. I mention this fact because the size of the vehicle is central to the story. It was a pretty little car, it had all the features of a toy racer, and I had fallen in love with it the first time I saw it on the lot.

In retrospect, I should have left it there.

Its English manufacturers, no doubt still seeing all of the colonies in the same latitude, had designed an automobile for little old ladies in Florida which they then decided to mail to the merciless young drivers of Newfoundland.

They had never seen a Newfoundland road of the time, much less driven over one, and had totally unprepared the Viva's fragile construction for the unexplored pothole terrain that passed for our Newfoundland road system of the time. Within weeks I had to replace parts that I had never heard of, much less pronounce with a Conception Bay accent.

My love affair with the little blue Viva ended just six months after purchase, and I traded it in on a much more solidly constructed Chevy product. This latter adaptation of a mini Russian tank treated the potholes with true mainland contempt, but needed the resources of two Arab emirates pumping daily just to keep it idling.

I never had much luck with cars.

That is the sad side of the story of the little blue Viva; but there were brighter moments, and the brightest, or at least the funniest, happened one day during March, St. Paddy's Day, in fact, and it happened right in my own driveway, which was what we were now calling that part of the yard just inside the gate. It was parked there while I killed some time waiting for the dance to begin at the Velvet Horn Club, which wouldn't be until ten o'clock.

You wouldn't have had to kill time like that ten years before, I'll guarantee you that. Then, dances started around eight o'clock. You pretty well had to walk everywhere you went, and that would sometimes mean an hour to the farthest communities. Before you set out you would need to spend a considerable amount of time washing the contours of your body with a very small cloth from an even smaller pan of water.

However, modern technology in the form of shower heads and automobiles had resolved these more primitive problems and provided us with immensely more time to waste and, by a strange quirk of social evolution, less time to dance at the same time.

However, we Newfoundlanders are an extraordinarily adaptable people, and have never refused the benefits of modernization, which in my case included a technological disaster for a car and nice new fancy labels on the same old black rum.

So there I was, sitting in the comfort of my parents' living room, celebrating the holiday in a leisurely sort of way. I had just finished clearing away the last of the snow from Sheila's Brush and was drinking hot black rum with sugar, pretending to stare at a black-and-white television so I wouldn't be staring at my very attractive neighbour who was sitting on the other end of the sofa.

We were roughly the same age, and years of visiting with her parents—who were friends of my parents—had fostered a mutual fondness which I continued to misinterpret as I grew older. Everybody else, including her, considered our being together as simple friendship, but in my case it was becoming serious temptation.

I mean, friendship was an appropriate word when she was eleven years old, missing front teeth, and throwing snowballs. At nineteen, outrageously good-looking from head to toe, and sitting just feet away on the same sofa, she was now, and could definitely become—as the old people would say—"cause for confession." Fortunately, I was mercifully rescued from the dangers of temptation by a thunderous stamping of feet and a roaring "Happy St. Patrick's Day to ye . . ." from the direction of the back porch—I'm sorry, the rear entrance.

* * * *

The reverberations along the canvas floor and through the warmth of the kitchen wood stove conveyed an image of something huge and powerful about to clomp into the kitchen, like an overweight Clydesdale or a very confused bull moose. I immediately had visions of Belle, the monstrous sheepish horse which my stepfather had bought the summer before, who insisted on coming straight into the kitchen if you weren't standing on cue on the doorstep with her daily ration of homemade bread and molasses.

Since I knew Belle was securely tethered in her stall contentedly munching oats—and since she had never been known to express good wishes to anybody in any language—the only other creature that I knew capable of making such a racket was Tiny Morton.

Tiny's real name was William Joseph Morton. He had been nicknamed Tiny in accordance with that transplanted, perverse Irish tradition which sought to draw attention to something by denoting its exact opposite. Tiny, by repute—nobody had ever weighed him, even at birth (they couldn't find a scale that could take the weight)—was three hundred and eighty-five pounds, and didn't extend upward so much as outward toward every known point of the compass, giving the onlooker the impression of a colossal molasses vat on tree trunks.

When you count the layers of clothes that his generation wore to keep warm and cover it all with a thick Arctic parka which had been sent by his son from Greenland, you can imagine that he had extreme difficulty navigating the narrow Newfoundland outport doors of the time.

Now I must declare at the beginning that one had absolutely nothing to fear from Tiny Morton, on St. Patrick's Day, or any other time, for that matter. Like most really big men, he seemed accepting of his size and strength, and he had never been known to lift a hand to anyone.

Tiny was your big old Newfoundland dog.

No doubt he could bark if he wanted to, but he was never known to. He just lived his life doing his work in his slow, easy way, rearing his family and minding his own business. Like most men of his generation, he worked hard at fish and woods and gardens, drank only on festive occasions, and moved among his neighbours quietly.

Except at times like St. Patrick's Day.

Then outport custom permitted him to leave his diminutive wife at home and "coast," as they used to describe it, from house to house, visiting and drinking and doing what today they call socializing. He could drink a puncheon, but he could hold his liquor, and he never got out of the way.

As a general rule with most outport men, what was in sober came out drunk. Which in most cases meant that you were sometimes surprised when a normally well-behaved gentleman of the community acted totally out of character and got on with a lot of stuff everybody would just as soon forget immediately thereafter. Like the time George Madden, the outport's really big merchant and a veritable pillar of the church—and a normally quiet, serious man—drank a full bottle of Saint Pierre rum, wrapped a big brin bag around his waist as a grass skirt—over his topcoat—held a mop behind his head to simulate hair, then stood on the coffee table and tried to emulate a hula dancer he once saw perform in New York—while the accordion was playing a step dance for Jimmy O'Toole, in front of a whole kitchen full of Christmas visitors.

In Tiny's case, it happened in reverse. The more he drank, the more cheerful he became. The normally surly look would disappear, his entire visage would soften, and he would become increasingly infused with an intense desire to enjoy himself.

Then, he would sing.

Not that people wanted him to, or asked him to, or encouraged him, like they would, say, Tom O'Reilly or Hannah O'Toole—they had voices like nightingales.

Those who had been unfortunate enough to have heard Tiny sing before fervently prayed that he would never sing again. But sing he would. He really loved to sing, and when he was drinking he desperately wanted to sing. The problem was that, for all the tea in China, he couldn't.

He didn't have a note to call his own.

When he did sing, in deference to his person and size, people respectfully listened, and the gathering tried as best they could to weather his contribution to the moment without losing their hearing—or their sanity—in the process.

Women crossed their arms and sat in patience, gently rocking to and fro, every now and then stroking their foreheads in silent prayer, while the men bowed their heads and muttered feigned encouragement, all the while exchanging anxious glances for fear that he would actually finish the song.

Thankfully, owing to his poor memory, the effects of the alcohol, and the length of the ballad in question, he rarely did. The older people said he used to do a tolerable job with "Johnny on the Reef" when he was younger, with its thirty-two verses and chorus after every verse and all that, but that was before my time.

There was no musical accompaniment to help him on—or drown him out, as the case might be. The accordion, like the violin, was only used for dancing, and the guitar, so prevalent today, had not yet caught on in Newfoundland homes.

Not that it would make any difference, since it would tax the combined talents of a roomful of European composers to follow the unpredictable cadences, abrupt time changes, and outright bellowing which constituted Tiny's rendering of any of his oft-sung repertoire.

When he was drunk, he loved to sing, but the stark fact remained that he couldn't. Yet, much to the despair of any hapless person unfortunate enough to be caught within kitchen space throughout the performance, he fervently insisted on doing so.

* * * *

So here he was, the full of our back porch, well on from tumblers of black rum he had just downed at Simon Flynn's, and bellowing like the siren of a coastal boat lost in the fog in Placentia Bay.

"A happy St. Patrick's Day to ye all," he roared, as he gripped the door facings from the outside in an effort to steady himself.

Being a basically polite man, he attempted to dislodge his number twelve–plus logans by alternately scrubbing his feet on the opposite leg, all the while swaying and plunging like a big freighter caught in a crosswind off Chalky Point. The fact that the logans were tightly laced to the top didn't deter him in the least, and he stood there for a considerable time making a genuine attempt to remove the snow-covered boots.

Having accomplished this objective to his satisfaction— the logans remained securely tied—he wedged himself with difficulty through the kitchen door, Arctic parka and all, and plopped down on the edge of the cushioned bench immediately inside the door, driving snow and snow water in every conceivable direction.

My parents and their guests went on playing a game of six-handed auction—where the dealer picks from the pack, and where my stepfather, God rest his soul, regularly placed the ace of hearts when he dealt—and I was left to tend to Tiny's wants. You may gather that they were not a whole lot different from the demands of any of the other male visitors who came to visit, except that in Tiny's case he didn't wait to be asked.

"Give me a drink of rum!" he roared.

For anybody unaware of his particular character, the effect would have been terrifying, three hundred and eighty-five pounds and all. For us it was, as the Americans on the bases called it, standard procedure. It was the way he was when he was drunk. He meant no more harm than if he were offering a head of cabbage from his fall garden.

"Give me a drink of rum," he ordered in the same bellowing tone. "I wants to wish ye a happy St. Patrick's Day."

He had doubtless forgotten that he had already expressed this wish a considerable number of times while he was trying to take off his logans in the back porch.

"We're goin' to have an early spring," he observed, totally changing his tone in the direction of the card players, who hadn't paid him the least attention up to this point, and who, for the duration of his visit, pretty well ignored him, a fact which didn't seem to bother Tiny in the least.

The kettle was still hot on the back of the stove, so I mixed him a regular drink of dark rum with hot water and sugar from the ingredients on the sideboard, and he took it with a monstrous unsteady arm, downing it at one gulp. Then, without any break or hesitation, he thrust the empty glass back to me with the same roaring demand, and, mindful of past Christmas experiences, I refilled the glass obediently, which disappeared in the same direction as fast as the first one.

Thrusting the glass back to me almost instantaneously, he roared a third time, "Give me another drink of rum, and I'll sing ye a song." For one fleeting moment, as the poets say, I thought of refusing, to spare myself what I knew would be certain torture, but I thought better of it—even if he shifted his weight he could hurt someone—and returned the glass to him a third time filled.

* * * *

He drained the glass of hot rum with the same backward bodily motion as before and returned the glass to me empty, declining my offer of a refill with a soft guttural sound and a wave of his big hand. He had drunk all three drinks in less time than I took to pour them, but that was it. Three drinks he wanted, three drinks he asked for, and three drinks he accepted, not one more. Then, true to his word, he announced his intention to sing, and a shudder could be observed around the card table.

As much as I dreaded it, I could only be a mournful victim of what was about to transpire.

"I'm going to sing ye a song now," he boomed. "I'm going to sing ye an auld Irish song. About a little b'y and his pore mudder."

Then, resting his big forearm on his thigh, he leaned his torso a bit to the right and began something that sounded like the dying wail of a tormented banshee, in a very, very, very loud voice.

It wasn't "Johnny on the Reef," but it was something akin to it, about the aforementioned "little b'y" and his "pore mudder," and I thought I understood the part where the boy left home when he was young, but that was as far as I got. I picked up a later reference to the "pore mudder's" heart breaking, but I couldn't be sure, and anyway it was somewhere in the eleventh verse, and by that time I had begun drinking big drinks of hot rum myself, out of sheer survival.

He swayed and thumped his fist on his knee, stamped his foot on the floor, and snapped his head sideways as if he were winking, while his body moved in unpredictable jerks and spasms thinking it was in time to the rhythm of the song, if indeed there was rhythm.

At one point he stood up and waved his cap in the air with great sweeping motions, shouting to the top of his voice all the while. We all thought he was going to dive headlong straight into the woodbox, but he regained his balance and sat down again without ever missing a word.

He slowed down considerably toward the end, becoming almost solemn as he pronounced the last seven words of the song—"As the pore young lad marched home." We all presumed "the pore young lad" had been to war and had come home safely to his mother, but none of us were really sure. Then he sat contentedly, looking very proud of himself, obviously waiting for some compliment from his victim audience.

True to their culture, the card players poured profuse adulation on his very energetic performance—in a totally detached manner—while at the same time concealing sighs of relief at the termination of what my stepfather would describe as "crucifying a song."

This contradiction between feeling and expression, considering the circumstance, they considered in no way hypocritical.

* * * *

The song over, Tiny straightened himself up and turned toward the door to leave. Probably overcome by the exertions of the day, or by the travails of the lad and his pore mudder, he turned to me and asked the question that turned the rest of the evening into the hilarious sideshow it became.

"Would you give me a ride up?" he asked, not considering the request in any manner out of the ordinary. "Me old legs are not what they used to be."

It was a sincere admission of the effects of a lot of work and a lot of age. For those of us who knew him, his sudden transformation into the quiet old Newfoundland dog once again was no surprise. In the final stage of Tiny's drinking, a stage where some other men would get loud and argumentative, even belligerent, Tiny merely got tired and sleepy, and wanted nothing better than to go back to his home and go to bed.

* * * *

That's when the little blue Viva re-entered the story.

It was all I had to offer to transport Tiny's three hundred and eighty-five–plus pounds, encased in layers of protective warm clothing and the bulky Arctic parka, and I could see problems looming on the horizon, or inside the car, whichever you prefer. My pretty neighbour had been just behind the living room door laughing her head off the whole time, and she laughed even harder when she heard the request.

She had her own sense of humour, and I suppose she was trying to envision Tiny's massive proportions jammed into the tiny little matchbox on wheels that did me fine at one hundred and thirty-five pounds. When I looked at her, I was envisioning other things, but the Butlers' catechism of my school days kept appearing as my walk-on conscience, and I had to content myself with asking her to accompany me to Tiny's house.

Deep down I hoped this would be the beginning of a successful ruse—like when you asked a girl at a parish hall dance if she wanted to go out to the door for some fresh air, and everybody, including the girl, knew exactly what you were asking. But for practical reasons I needed somebody with me.

Escorting home a drunken man in a Newfoundland outport of the time—if you weren't the police—was fraught with its own dangers, principally from the drunken man's wife, who invariably blamed the one escorting him for having made her husband drunk, irrespective of the true facts of the case.

So the trick was to have an excuse to leave the situation as quickly as you could. So I made it up with my pretty neighbour to demand that I leave on a prearranged signal.

That way I could play the polite taxi driver, not offend my potential host, or get too heavy a scarafunging from an over-angry Newfoundland wife, all in the bargain. If everything worked according to plan, there would still be time to show my pretty neighbour the Lookout and investigate the freshness of the air at that altitude.

We both dressed for the outdoors and followed Tiny, or attempted to follow Tiny, as he weaved his way through the back porch. He glanced down to ensure that his logans were on, having forgotten entirely about his unsuccessful attempts to take them off earlier, made a feeble attempt to draw his parka tighter around him—it just wasn't big enough—then stepped unsteadily onto the large Kelly's Island rock that served as a back step, aiming himself in the general direction of the little blue Viva.

"Where's the car?" he slurred, looking over the little vehicle directly ahead of him. Subconsciously, even he was anticipating problems.

"Right in front of you, Mr. Morton," I replied graciously, terrified at that point that he might step on the car by mistake. He would have done a lot of damage.

We guided him toward the vehicle, one on each side trying to support him, which presented its own unforeseen problem. Every time he lurched my knees buckled as I tried to support his weight. I had visions of crumpling to the snow under the human tonnage, never to be found again. The fact that my pretty neighbour would be somewhere on top in the distant height, having being dragged down herself from the other side, was no consolation, since, at this point, she would be too far up in the air to be of any romantic value.

We stopped beside the door on the passenger side, where I again contemplated the size of the problem which loomed up in front of us, or between us, again, whichever you prefer. Simple observation told me that the car was much too small, and Tiny was much too big. I scratched my head with an unsteady hand as I racked my brain for some simple solution.

There was none.

We would simply have to get him into the car the best way we could, so we pointed him in the direction of the open door, then set out to manoeuvre him into the front seat, pushing and straining with all our might. The only help that Tiny could give us was to co-operate with the downward attraction of gravity as he toppled forward in the direction we were pushing.

Gravity, however, proved to be too helpful.

Our last determined thrust got him forward, but, as the outport wit would say, not forward enough. Tiny got stuck; his massive bulk solidly wedged between the doorposts of the car, his feet with the number twelve–plus logans resting securely on the outside. We tugged in every which way we could, in a vain attempt to dislodge him, but the effect was the same as the efforts of two very small mice trying to displace a very large elephant.

Tiny didn't budge an inch.

Meanwhile, we were more than happy he wasn't getting upset, and were congratulating ourselves on our not upsetting or provoking him by our continued futile efforts.

A loud, long, drawn-out snoring from inside the car told us we need not have worried. Tiny, having totally succumbed to the effects of the alcohol and the exertions of the afternoon, and having found a position of relative comfort to rest his tired mind and body, had fallen sound asleep.

We were faced at this point with what my learned friend at the university would call "somewhat of a conundrum." Since we couldn't get Tiny in any farther, we had to get him all the way out in order to get him all the way back in again—try the attempt, as it were, from some other vantage point.

My pretty neighbour was no help. She was already past the point of hysterics, resting her head on her elbows on the car to keep from falling to the ground from sheer laughter. She eventually summoned up enough energy to detach herself from that position and find her way around to the other side and, as it turned out, provide a solution to our mutual problem.

She positioned herself on the front seat, then pushed with all her might on Tiny's snoring head as I tugged with all my might on his parka from the opposite direction.

You have to give the modern outport woman credit for unbelievable strength. Tiny came free, but he didn't exactly ease back gently and thank us in polite tones. My pretty neighbour, perhaps unschooled in the laws of physics that govern such instances—large bodies in motion tend to travel very fast and that sort of thing—pushed with such force that she sent Tiny hurtling from the car like a rhinoceros catapulted from a gigantic slingshot. I just had time to dive into the bank of snow by the porch door to escape instant obliteration.

I watched from the snowbank as the solidity of the porch and the immensity of Tiny met each other by the clapboard walls, shielding my eyes against the splinters that would emerge from the explosive contact and envisioning the large hole that would result. However, the house had been built solidly, with thick, rinded spruce for uprights, and except for a minor shuddering of the building on impact—and a bit of shaking on the foundations—not a piece of wood cracked.

The only real damage that occurred was the interruption with the card game inside. My stepfather at that point was in the act of dealing, and the unexpected jolt had sent the cards flying across the table. He had to reshuffle the deck a second time to ensure that the ace of hearts was again on the bottom of the deck.

However, the impact did create another problem for us on the outside. To his drunken and confused mind, the collision with the porch was nothing less than a treacherous blow from behind, and Tiny immediately assumed he was in a fight.

Fortunately, he didn't pick a human target as his intended opponent, as an angry, drunken fighter might do. He merely stood in one spot in front of the porch, growling and grumbling menacingly to everything and everyone within earshot, and flailing his arms like a giant windmill about to become airborne, generating air currents that stirred up snow across the yard.

My pretty neighbour interrupted her laughing long enough to ease between the flailing arms and encourage him toward the car, all the while speaking in soothing tones and essentially returning him to the big old Newfoundland dog he always was.

* * * *

We finally got him in the car, got the door closed with difficulty, and except for the fact that Tiny once again fell asleep in the warmth of the car and snored all the way home, driving the short distance to his house was uneventful. We arrived at his yard beneath Cooper's Mountain, got him out with surprisingly little difficulty, and helped him to the door of his little saltbox.

Tiny's diminutive wife must have been equipped with that

new sonar. She was waiting in the open door, arms akimbo, ready to take on a regiment.

Years of weightlifting had not prepared me for the moment.

Her greeting was typical of the transplanted Irish Newfoundland woman.

"Well, you great bitches' divil . . . ?"

It didn't help that she was looking at both of us, and I was glad the pretty neighbour was with me. At that point I could forgo the immoral aspirations for some simple female protection. Tiny's wife was only a small woman, but I had heard too many stories of little people throwing bigger people off the head of the wharf.

Fortunately, in that respect, she and Tiny were well-matched. Neither were capable of hurting or harming a fly. Once she felt she had performed her dutiful condemnatory ritual at the door and Tiny, towering over her, had muttered something in an apologetic tone about "just coastin' . . ." she turned and beckoned all three of us in.

∗ ∗ ∗ ∗

Once inside the house, rum and hot water were produced—sherry wine and dark fruitcake for my pretty neighbour—and we were treated royally indeed. Tiny, now wide awake after his two short naps, acted as host. He didn't sing, although he did recount a number of stories about pirates and Irish "rogues" and how the priest hid on the British soldiers back in 1756 and all of that, and so long as he was supplying the hot rum I was ready to believe the stories.

In fact, I was having such a good time that I forgot all about my prearranged plan to leave early. When my pretty neighbour started winking and nodding her head in the direction of the door, I thought she was finally hinting at going out for some fresh air. Inwardly ecstatic at the turn things had taken in my direction, I hurriedly gulped my last drink of rum and followed her to the car.

I needn't have rushed. She was only interested in going to the dance. Which was just as well. What with all that snow we had dumped on us by Sheila's Brush, they probably didn't have the road to the Lookout plowed, and I'd had enough fresh air for one night, anyway.

We went on to the dance at the Velvet Horn, as I had intended at the beginning and, as they used to say about the bean suppers in the social notes on radio a spell ago, a good time was had by all.

* * * *

It's a long time ago since I had that little blue Viva, which no doubt by now is well consigned to rusty oblivion, and if it wasn't for Tiny Morton, I'd have nothing but bad memories of that little car.

Both Tiny and his wife are dead now, God rest their souls.

He got sick a year or so after that, and he died while I was teaching along the coast. His little wife died not too long after. That St. Patrick's Day was the last time I heard him sing. Funny thing is, for all his bellowing and stomping, for a long time after I missed his annual visit.

Mind you, for all my nostalgia, I still don't know if I could endure another verse of that "little b'y and his pore mudder"; but that's the crazy thing about Newfoundland. You don't want it when it's there, but you miss it when it's not there, and you'll search through all God's creation to find it and bring it back the way it was when it's gone.

Oh, we have all kinds of tapes and records and discs, and

the best sound systems that money can buy, and every kind of fancy singer doing songs on radio and television you'd want to listen to, but every so often I get to thinking about Tiny Morton, and I feel a little sad. It's like all those other nice things in the past that have gone and will simply never come back.

My pretty neighbour? Oh, she fell in love with a Mountie who drove a big fancy Chrysler. The last I heard they had gotten married and moved up to Canada.

They say the air is much fresher up there.

THE LAW OF THE OCEAN

The law of the ocean is ruthless
It crushes the creature at will
It knows neither age nor high station
Its hunger for death's never still

From Cape Race, Cape Anguille to Cape Chidley
Their names are carved into stone
On great ships they went down in great numbers
Yet they could—and they did—die alone

Were they known, like Sir Humphrey Gilbert
Great men of history, of fame?
Or were they buried on some lonely coastline
Without even a cross for their name?

Were their ships crushed and strewn o'er the
    coastline?
(The fate of the sad *Florizel*)
Were they granted some brief glimpse of heaven
While facing their storm-ridden hell?

Did they die in some great sealing disaster
Their faces frozen in tears?

While the storm howled and shrieked in its fury
Cut down in the prime of their years

Or was it some man-made disaster
That came with death from afar?
With torpedoes and great conflagration ·
The *Caribou*, all those ships lost in war

Were they children, playing on ice pans
Secure and safe by the beach?
Till they slipped, and the power sucking under
Dragged them to death beyond reach

I study a map by my window
Names of schooners (by the hundreds) in blocks
The *Cora*, the *Ruby*, the *Rosie* . . .
Storm-ravaged on Newfoundland's rocks

Were the names a wife or a daughter
Left home to await their return?
The *Myrtle*, the *Nellie*, *Vanessa* . . .
Left home forever to mourn

Forever to mourn and walk sadly
To a church to kneel and to pray
For a loved one whose grave is the ocean
Where he lies for heaven to say

To walk with a face etched in sorrow
Dress in black as they did in past days
Or sit in a chair by the window
In memory to dream . . . and to gaze . . .

I too turn my head back in sorrow
At numbers that darken my mind
And I turn from the pages of history
To leave the darkness behind

But the darkness remains in the present
From an ocean we can't seem to shun
Its yearning for sorrow unfinished
The *Ranger*, Flight Four Ninety-one . . .

Draggers and crab boats and trawlers
Does it matter the size or the kind?
When they're lost? The *Myers III*, the *Sea Gypsy*
There are always loved ones left behind

We're a people surrounded by ocean
An ocean we can't seem to spurn
It gives of its bounty unending
But demands its own price in return

The pages of history are crowded
With the names of those who've been lost
But we will go on till it's ended
No matter the trial or the cost

We'll follow the way of the ocean
As we've done since our hist'ry began
Rememb'ring all those gone before us
Every brave woman and man

FEATHERS IN THE SOUP

Aunt Maude Finnegan's rooster was dead.

Dead as a doornail. Killed on a beautiful Sunday afternoon in July, would you believe. Killed by "that blood-uv-a-bitch of a Tommy Shannigan, going mad around the corner" as Aunt Maude would describe the event later. And the said "blood-uv-a-bitch" didn't apologize or say he was sorry or utter one word of condolence to Aunt Maude on her grievous loss or give her one red cent in the bargain.

Certainly, killing a rooster at that point wasn't Tommy's biggest problem. A new police force was now present in the outports of Newfoundland, and they didn't look kindly on people like Tommy Shannigan going mad around corners in big cars, causing havoc on outport roads. In fact, the Mounties had a very unforgiving approach toward this kind of Newfoundland behaviour since their arrival in the province, and were determined to make the roads safe for other sensible drivers, as few in number as they were.

And what a rooster!

The very pride of Merry Harbour. Big and red and majestic, with an ancestry that went back to those fierce cock-fighting days of yesteryear, unchallenged in the barnyard as the undisputed lord of thirteen hens, strutting back and forth among his mini harem like a newly elected politician who has just bought his wife an expensive fur coat.

And now he was dead.

Not that his killing was the most tragic event that could have happened in the small outport of Merry Harbour. Over the years, other equally tragic events had occurred that merited the attention of the residents, even dwarfed the death of the rooster by comparison.

There was the time Mrs. Malarky left her good curtains on the line to air when she was spring cleaning and a huge bull moose that up to now everybody had thought quite friendly showed up to chew the lace off the edges. Then there was the time Jack Hennessey and the lads put Jake Murphy's pig in the back of the Muckler's brand new car while he was in Mahaney's store and the Muckler drove around Merry Harbour for two hours wondering why the new engine was burning oil. And of course everybody remembers the time the squids rolled ashore behind the point and got trapped at low tide and were so terribly transformed by the hottest August we ever had . . .

But, sir, for sheer fun and entertainment, none of them could touch the killing of the rooster on that beautiful summer afternoon.

Tommy Shannigan killed him, that "young blood-uv-a-bitch," out tearing around the roads in a big De Soto on a beautiful Sunday afternoon when he should have been in church praying instead of flying low frightening people to death.

And well you may ask, "Pray tell, why is the killing of a big, red outport rooster of such importance in the chronicles of Newfoundland history when set beside other momentous events like French invasions and the depredations of people like Peter Easton and terrible fish prices and that sort of thing?" Well, Aunt Maude, the aforesaid owner of the rooster, was robbed of her Christmas dinner, six months hence, that's the importance. Her only rooster, the rooster she was saving for Christmas, plucked out of existence, out of her pot, so to speak, never to brighten her Christmas table.

And how can a rooster assume such importance? Well, when you're a widow in the days before Confederation subsisting on twelve-fifty a quarter, you needed all the help you could get, and, for widows, things didn't change much after Confederation. So Aunt Maude had her little garden and her few hens to eke out her existence as best she could, in a time when money was as scarce as the teeth of the hens she reared.

The big, red rooster was her pride and glory. She had always guarded him like a hawk—the local lads were always stealing hens for soup—(and being promoted to high positions in the RCMP later on for their accomplishments)—but today she had imprudently left her yard gate open. This gave an unwilling black hen the chance to escape the unwanted advances of a very willing and flirtatious rooster; and gave the rooster the chance of flirting with death first-hand instead of with the unwilling black hen.

And that's when Tommy Shannigan entered the story. "Flying low" around the corner, going as fast as he could to get absolutely nowhere in jig time, he had to swerve to avoid the two big maples on one side of the road, lost control of the vehicle—if he had any up to this point—and hit J. J. Mahaney's shop on the other side.

And not only hit the shop! He went right through the shop. The most prestigious shop in Merry Harbour—the biggest, reddest shop in Cobbler's Bay—and he went right through the corner, in through one big picture window and out through the other, spewing glass in every direction.

And it didn't stop there. The car, I mean. Assuming that it had complete control of the situation, as it had had for some time, and undeterred by what it considered as nothing more than a minor setback to its errant escapade, it barrelled across the gravel parking space like one of those modern-day rockets, hell-bent on destroying everything in its path.

J. J. Mahaney's solitary green and white gas tank, which, ruefully, happened to be directly in its path, was set flying, landing somewhere among the white rose bushes in the south side of the garden. Three lengths of new, white paling fence were totally eliminated, and Mrs. Mahaney's superbly cultivated patch of tame strawberries, which the lads of the parish had not yet had the good fortune to rob, received its first unwelcome visitor.

Then, after spinning wildly for a few seconds, driving strawberries like a top spinning, it emerged from the garden through the same passage it had created in the fence on its way through, somewhat slowed by its encounter with the deep, soft clay of the strawberry patch. As if in sorrow for the wanton destruction it had caused, it re-entered the gravel parking area with its momentum substantially reduced, terminating its turbulent adventure by parking timidly in the middle of the road, unremorseful about the damage and chaos it had wrought—its young driver still gripping the steering wheel at arm's length, rigid with fright from the experience.

The big, red rooster got killed on the way back, not on the way toward the strawberry patch, as some later argued. Like many a male the world over, he died in amorous pursuit of a female of his species, in this case a little black hen. The latter had sprinted some distance ahead of her pursuer and thereby avoided injury herself, but the big, red rooster, in his haste to catch up, collided with the corner of the bumper of Tommy's big De Soto on its return trip through the fence. Given the advantages of modern technology, the collision was immensely in favour of the De Soto, and the big, red rooster was sent flying through the air, and, for the first time, not of his own accord.

He landed in an upright position in front of the broken gas pump, where he stood for some time totally motionless, obviously dazed by the blow and seemingly perplexed at this sudden and horrific turn of events in his life. Then, after wobbling to and fro for another short time, possibly overwhelmed by the accompanying fear of imminent and unexpected death, he dropped on his back and gave up his spirit in much the same way as one of those poorer actors in a second-rate movie death scene. There he lay in his waking position, the concrete base of the gas pump providing him with a ready-made tombstone, the red feathers which were shed from his body on impact, and up to now had been floating rather aimlessly in the wind, settling gently around his sorrowful corpse, like roses at a Mafia funeral.

The little black hen, meanwhile, having obviously severed any emotional ties which might have existed with the rooster up to this point, and totally unperturbed by the violent events of the afternoon which had unfolded around her, was pecking abstractedly in the strawberry patch, the soul of content in the middle of all the near-ripe strawberries.

The plot, or the broth, whichever you prefer, now began to thicken.

The villain, Tommy Shannigan, emerged from the car slowly, a look of shock upon his young face as he surveyed the devastation effected by his wild escapade. The car was a brand new De Soto that he had purchased just a week before with money he had saved from two stints on an American base in Greenland, and he had cared for it like you would a baby. Now it stood scratched, dented, bruised, and covered with dirt, testimony to the errant behaviour of its remorseful owner, who stood resting on the open car door, letting the full weight of his transgression settle over him.

One could never condone his actions, of course, and there were many in the gathering crowd who were quick to condemn, but to be fair, it could be argued that he had done no more than succumb to the twin vices of youth and bad judgment, which seems to be the general problem with young people the world over, of whatever era, especially where big, fast, shiny new cars are concerned.

From this perspective, he had succumbed to the temptation of his time, which in this case consisted of getting as much speed as possible out of a big eight-cylinder engine in a heavy car on a narrow, winding gravel road with very little experience as a driver, and he was now paying the price. He hadn't had the benefit of driver training programs which are so much in vogue today—what preparation he had consisted of three practice runs in his uncles's land rover—and had been given his licence after only two supervised runs on Blackduck Hill without stalling the standard transmission and rolling back.

The rooster, of course, being dead, hadn't moved in all this time, but was still the centre of attention for the gathering crowd, which had appeared from nowhere and constituted a relatively large number, when you consider the size of the outport. It was Sunday afternoon, and anybody who was anybody—certainly everybody who was within hearing distance of the racket—had rushed to the scene, having abandoned knitting needles and playing cards and hay prongs in favour of hurrying to the accident scene, so as not to miss out on any of the anticipated excitement. They arranged themselves in standing-room-only fashion in concentric rings around the scene, jostling and craning to obtain the most advantageous point from which to view—and enjoy—the upcoming proceedings.

With the crowd and Tommy settled into their respective roles, what remained to complete the cast for the continuing scenes would be the entrance of the RCMP, who were sure to respond to every accident on the corner on Sundays, and the arrival of Aunt Maude, who, being the owner of the dead bird, could be deemed the most tragic character in the play, assuming the lead role, if you will, and who should have elicited the most sympathy.

Neither were long in coming.

Within moments a police car screamed to a halt, siren wailing as if warning of yet another impending French invasion, and disgorged a lone police officer, his youthful appearance bespeaking his inexperience in the field, having been sent to Newfoundland on his first posting under the assumption that he wouldn't have a whole lot of crime to deal with, anyway. There were very few cars outside the city in those years, mainly because there were very few roads outside the city, and there wasn't a lot of stealing and stuff like that because most people in those days really didn't have much worth taking, anyway.

He was not at all prepared for his first real foray into Newfoundland outport culture, a culture which had experienced enough seriousness in hardship and hard times and tuberculosis and such that another Sunday accident on Kayten's Corner was nothing more than a harmless opportunity for a little conversation and a much-needed bit of fun.

Neither was he prepared for a confrontation with a Newfoundland widow who had lived through two world wars and a terrible depression, buried two husbands, and who, for seventy-two years, had survived—almost entirely through her own wit and ingenuity—the sicknesses, troubles, and general hardship that has gone a long way to make up the romantic Newfoundland past.

Aunt Maude didn't arrive on the scene as much as she descended on it, something like a hurricane blast of wind in an October gale, cowing and flattening everything in its path, like the "roaring savage," as the old folks would say. She was tall and raw-boned, straight as a whip in spite of her seventy-two years, and could turn hay or hoe out potatoes with the best of them, men or women, in her younger days. Even at her advanced age, she still brought in her own wood and tended her garden, and pretty well looked after herself.

So what suddenly emerged centre stage onto the accident scene was no syrupy-sweet '50s movie heroine ready to faint at a lover's sigh, but an enraged Newfoundland widow whose sole purpose in life at the moment was to wreak vengeance on whoever robbed her of her forthcoming Christmas dinner.

For such, as I have said, was the rooster's hallowed destiny.

The big, red rooster was her prime accomplishment over the past year or so. She had fattened him with care and patience, and was secretly looking forward to next Christmas Day when she could bake him and garnish him and proudly serve him to the three other ladies who came to visit her and who formed, with her, what you would call today a social club.

Consistent with the practical turn of the people of her day, she had no particular or personal attachment to the fowl, as women have today for, say, corgis or French poodles. However, she had been fattening him up to display as Christmas Day dinner, and the fact that she could still salvage the remains for immediate consumption did not in any way counter the despair she would experience at the thought of her rooster's absence from the table on that festive date.

Neither would it replace the compliments which her three visiting friends would heap on her for raising such a clever bird, ample reward in a culture craving little materially, but, like human beings the world over, needing all the credit they could get for whatever small achievements they could attain in the harried obscurity of their daily lives.

Enraged that she would be denied the pleasure of witnessing her rooster in the pot on Christmas Day, she doubtless concluded that his killer would do just as well on that particular Sunday afternoon.

The neighbour who brought her the news had caught her in the act of scouring her iron skillet, which up to now had been utilized in peaceful fashion to cook the weekly allocation of fresh meat and gravy purchased the day before from the Protestant meat man, and she had absent-mindedly carried it with her in her haste to reach the scene of the accident.

She readily espied Tommy Shannigan, who at this point was being guided to the police car for questioning, and, as such, made an easy target for her wrath. Bearing down upon Tommy in his vulnerable state, she appeared fully intent upon burying the iron skillet in his unprotected skull.

That she didn't was due solely to the timely intervention of the RCMP officer who saw her coming, and who was so intent on courageously protecting Tommy's skull from the murderous utensil that he came darn near close to having it buried in his own. Aunt Maude still had enough of the blood of her Celtic ancestors to wield the iron skillet like a broadsword in battle, and the young Mountie had to weave and duck with genuine alacrity to dodge the great swinging arcs of the bloodthirsty skillet.

To be fair, Aunt Maude had nothing in particular against Mounties—or any other law enforcement agency, for that matter. (She had almost married the local constable many years before.) She was merely attempting to render an eye for an eye, or an outport taxi driver for a rooster, or fulfilling whatever legal maxim her angered sense of legal justice was dictating during that frenzied moment.

However, in the immortal words of Sir Winston, she would be denied her finest hour. Or at least partially so, since the new RCMP constable did give both himself and Aunt Maude a small degree of notoriety when he accidentally tore her blouse, while attempting to wrestle the skillet from her hands, in a desperate attempt at self-defence.

Seeking to avoid yet another impending blow of the cooking utensil turned assault weapon, he lunged to grab the frying pan but grabbed instead the lapel of Aunt Maude's blouse just below the neckline, ripping the blouse slightly and exposing a rather large but not unattractive portion of bright red flannelette.

Though she was doubtless well-protected by numerous such layers of like flannelette, as was the prevailing custom of the older ladies of her era—to keep out the heat, as they said—the rend in the garment protecting her bosom did little to calm the rage boiling within that well-protected part of her anatomy.

With a scream like a wounded banshee, she lunged with all her might at this brazen intruder into her inner sanctity. Fortunately, the RCMP officer tripped over Tommy Shannigan's bumper and fell backwards on the bonnet of the car, while Aunt Maude went flying across the parking area onto the gravel, propelled by the weight of the skillet, which she still gripped vehemently in both hands.

There she was finally subdued and soothed by the collective intervention of her three friends who had rushed to the scene upon hearing of the calamity, just in time to prevent serious injury to that hapless enforcer of the law.

Her friends helped Aunt Maude to her feet, where she stood for a moment panting and sweating, swaying with fatigue from the intense exertion. The fuming and flailing instigated by the tear in the outer layer of her apparel, and her efforts to repay the RCMP constable for his part as violator, had totally exhausted her and forced her, albeit unwillingly, to disengage from the fray, something that would have been unthinkable on her part twenty years before.

With a final savage look toward Tommy Shannigan—a look which was totally lost on him owing to his state of all-consuming terror—she gave her torso a savage twist, then strode, fuming silently, toward the gate in her yard. The crowd parted before her, much like the Red Sea in *The Ten Commandments*, and she dealt them vicious looks left and right in gratitude.

Halfway across the road, however, as if prompted by some unknown spirit of malevolence, she stopped abruptly, swung about-face and, with strides more suited to the charge of an angry bull moose, arrived by the side of the unmoving rooster, who, to give him his credit, had been a most unwilling cause of the events at hand.

Seething with spite at not being able to crush Tommy Shannigan's skull with her iron frying pan, she proceeded, totally inexplicably, to vent her unsatiated rage on the luckless form of the dead rooster, having reversed the order of justice to which she had thus far been adhering.

Forgetting her previous role of advocate and protector, she now delivered the dead bird such a kick that he flew over the fence, landing with an unexcitingly dull thump right in the middle of the strawberry patch, where he was studiously ignored by the little black hen, absorbed as she was in the more pressing demand of gobbling up all the strawberries that she could before she was rounded up again and returned to the relative monotony of the hen's pound.

Someone in the crowd who had seen a football game while they were in the 'States avowed that a kick like that deserved a contract, but he had no intentions of offering her one in her present state of mind.

She then strode angrily into her house, without even so much as a farewell glance in her rooster's direction. Once inside, the inner surroundings of her bungalow would endure the final expression of her wrath through the medium of assorted slammed doors and smashed dishes, the big grey cat having prudently exited to the safety of a neighbour's shed.

Her departure signalled the end of her role in the public entertainment, and, with Tommy settled in the police car awaiting questioning, the crowd began to disperse, the more serious component drifting back to home or wharf or whatever duties of the afternoon, the less scrupulous having already formed a plan in their collective minds, a plan that included the dead rooster as the chief ingredient.

In that sense, Aunt Maude's obvious disavowal of the dead bird turned out to be a unique stroke of luck. These fellows knew good fortune when they saw it, although they weren't high on that kind of articulation, and could readily seize upon the opportunity to have chicken soup, and a time to boot, without having to submit to the hazards of climbing over manure piles at the backs of stables to steal the chief ingredient for the pot.

The rooster was unceremoniously seized by an onlooker with the most assertive leadership qualities—the most brazen, as they would say then—and carried by the legs in an inconceivably undignified manner to a house immediately adjacent to the accident scene.

Friends and accomplices made up a mock funeral cortège as they followed him, singing a very bad rendition of "Nearer My God to Thee" in solemn tones in anticipation of the rooster's final farewell.

The house in question was the residence of a very ordinary older couple who made prodigious use of the moonshine can and had established a bit of a reputation for themselves in the community thereby. The lads hung out here on a regular basis till all hours of the night, moonshine was available for purchase by the half-pint bottle, and it was widely suspected— but never proven—that many a stolen hen had ended its days in the owner's boiler.

In the outport Newfoundland of the day, it was the closest thing you got to a house of ill repute.

* * * *

Once inside, the soup-making ritual began.

The big, red rooster was meticulously cleaned and dropped, again unceremoniously, into a large boiler, where his proud career as centre of attraction to the female members of his flock ended among assorted pieces of carrot and parsnip, and, as they say, "rice accardin." Copiously seasoned, the object of admiration of countless hens ended his days as the culinary centre of an old-time "kitchen racket."

As the once glorious rooster was ravenously devoured, and the sounds of slurping soup resounded among the kitchen walls, tumblers of hot moonshine were passed around. An accordion came out of nowhere. There was soon singing and step-dancing, and what began as a small-time scoff escalated into a first-rate party.

The events of the day were told and retold into the wee hours of the morning, a telling and retelling which would only cease when the soup and moonshine were both exhausted, and nothing would remain of the rooster except some unrecognizable bones which would be ignominiously thrown on the manure pile the next day.

The b'ys were short on metaphysics and teleology, but they

knew enough about life and death to understand the final end of a fattened rooster, and they didn't bother themselves about philosophy and suchlike while hot chicken soup and moonshine were still in abundance on the table. These people didn't have to wait for fast-food outlets to teach them how to value cooked chicken, although the new health regulations would have said a thing or two about feathers in the soup.

Many a smiling comment was passed about Aunt Maude's unfortunate loss, to the accompaniment of generous rounds of raucous laughter. As befitted the social role of her ponderous presence, such comments were disapprovingly hush-hushed by the ruling matriarch of the household, who outwardly disclaimed against the pilfering of the bird and vocalized her sympathies for Aunt Maude accordingly, but who inwardly couldn't wait for the first taste of the delectable broth.

* * * *

It's been a long time since that big, red rooster so ignominiously departed from this world.

Sadly, Aunt Maude Finnegan followed soon after in his wake, no pun intended. Her passing was not in any way related to the tragic demise of her favourite rooster. However, because her body was found peacefully asleep in somewhat the same position as that of the rooster's in much unhappier circumstances, the local wits, aping the daily newspapers which were now finding their way with more alacrity into outport households, seriously and solemnly affirmed that no foul play was suspected.

The matriarch who presided over the ritualistic scoff has also departed this world, and she, along with all those of her generation, have taken a world with her.

Mind you, we have a million channels on television and

all the world news we can eat. And I wouldn't want any of that stuff back—the muddy roads, the little wood stove in the corner, taking a beach rock to bed to keep your feet warm—most definitely not. I'm more sensible than that. I'm a lot better off and a darn sight more comfortable than they ever were.

It's just that—well—they seemed to have more fun.

TOMORROW THE GILLER

"What are you writing now?" asked my wife as she squinted over my shoulder.

"A novel," I replied, with absolute confidence.

"A novel! But I thought you were writing a short story."

She was furrowing her brows, not sure if she had heard me correctly. I knew she was doing all this behind me, because I had seen her do it before in that exact same tone of voice. She always squints first, then furrows after.

"Yes, short stories lack the depth of the profound life experience. It says so right here in the *Central Avalon Peninsula Author's Guide for Beginner Writers*."

"Profound life experience?"

My wife sounded skeptical.

"Yes, a short story could never fully express my profound life experience . . . where I was a teacher all those years . . . then there was that time I went to Saint Pierre . . ."

"You started a novel eight years ago?"

It was definitely a mild reprimand. My wife didn't like things dragged out.

"Yes. This is another one. I'm going to write both of them concurrently. The *Guide* says it can sometimes be the best way to overcome writer's block. If you're having trouble with the first novel, begin a second one."

My wife was pursing her lips with her fingers.

"If you can't write one, write two. Isn't that . . . ?"

"It might be, but I'm inclined to agree with them. Besides, maybe I can write them so they follow one another . . . like a trilogy."

My wife was looking at me as if she didn't understand, her eyes narrowing even more than she had previously furrowed. She was incredibly sensitive to my creative moods.

"A trilogy has three books."

"Yes, I know that. I will write these two concurrently and the third will naturally arise from the intense flow of creativity to which I have subjected myself writing the first two."

"But you only wrote two chapters of that first novel; the Train and the Boat. You didn't even finish the third chapter— The Kitchen."

"Yes, these were the symbolic representations of Newfoundland outport life."

"But you had the awfulest time with them."

"What do you mean?"

It was my turn to furrow. I never squinted, although sometimes I looked piercingly.

"Well, you only ever had two characters, and they were ever so long in one place. For the longest time you couldn't get them off the boat. And they're still in the kitchen!"

"An absolutely disciplined approach. You remember Lawrence Durrell. They all sat around a table in Cairo through four books. He only had four characters. Cleo . . ."

"I know them," she interrupted. Of course she did. My wife has read more novels than I could ever write in a year.

"But he was a distinguished European writer, like Joseph Conrad. He . . ."

I stopped her, showing mild displeasure in return.

"Joseph Conrad had to write in a foreign language."

"You could write in Polish?"

My wife was shaking her head in amazement. She always expressed amazement at my wide-ranging knowledge of literature.

"Of course, if I sailed around on Polish ships for a while."

Now she was shaking her head in absolute disbelief.

"You should finish your first novel before you do anything else."

That's what *she* would do. Every author has a different approach. The *Central Avalon Peninsula Author's Guide for Beginner Writers* was very clear on that.

"Besides, I can't think of any more symbolic representations of Newfoundland life."

I sat musingly.

"What about the wharf?"

I could have sworn the tone was acerbic, but I interpreted it as helpful. I thought a moment before I replied.

"No, the wharf would never work. The heroine has high heel shoes on—spike heels. They would get caught up in the spaces between the planks. She would trip and get hurt and I don't know how to write about hospitals . . ."

The *Guide* said a beginner writer had to be authentic.

"Besides, they would be standing there too long—for a whole chapter—and we're getting into late fall . . . winter. And they would have to change clothes. I would have to rewrite pages. I have to maintain consistency. That's what the *Guide* says."

That got her. Imagine using the wharf for a symbolic representation of Newfoundland life! My wife straightened and the lines of her face tautened. Her voice had taken on an unusually dry tone.

"Maybe they wouldn't have to talk at all. Maybe she could just stand there and have her coat furl around her aching legs while he tried to haul her out from between the planks."

I should have picked up on the tone more quickly, but I was becoming excited, my inspiration triggered by my wife's metaphorical language. Burst upon burst of creative energy flooded through my brain, unleashing images like the thick rolling of the sea. The images tumbled over one another like potheads roiling in shallow water by a deserted beach.

"Excellent," I shouted. "A beautiful metaphor. Furl. Just like a sail. The nautical reference. You're absolutely right. I should go back to my first novel. Splendid. 'Her thin coat furling around her aching legs . . . while squid-shaped forms danced on the harbour stillness.' That's it. Authenticity. Keep it Newfoundland. Precise detail. That's what the *Guide* says. . . . Or should I say 'Her squid-shaped coat . . . swirling sail-like. I have to be more precise. . . . Let's see . . . sail-like, sail-like . . .'"

The door was closing quietly. I was alone, with my genius, my inspiration. Every Central Avalon Beginner Writer should have such an encouraging and knowing wife, to help him past his first Beginner Writer's Block, to help him recognize the infinite limits of his bursting imagination. I was typing furiously.

"She stood on the wharf, a slippery wharf, a wharf of many planks, with spaces in between, with one plank missing (probably stolen); her loose-fitting Arcade-purchased coat furling and reefing about her tautened, aching legs . . . the anguished squirting of many squids the only sound to disturb the ethereal silence of an excitingly demure August afternoon . . ."

Perfect! Now what will I have him say first . . . ? I know, the sexual reference. Just a hint of sexual overture.

"Astrophilia, my dear, you look so beautiful standing on a planked wharf, your coat so sail-like, furling and reefing . . ."

HE WAS A MINER

He sits, a tired man, beside his stove
Drawing warmth from the little that remains
His memories begin with that small cove
With its rippling brooks and gentle, winding
    lanes

"I was just fifteen" (He coughed a wracking cough)
"You went to work, there were no choices then
Well, join the church . . . fish. . . . Times were bad
If you had a lot of learning wield a pen"

He drew his breath in hard. "I had no berth
And you have but little learning with grade eight
Join the Church?" He smiled amidst his pain
"I don't think I was made for Heaven's gate"

"No, the mines had everything you'd ask"
(He paused to stem another wracking cough)
"Just pick and shovel, bend hard to the task
And as for pay, well, they paid enough"

"You name one, I've been there . . . I've dug it all . . .
Lead in Buchans, Tilt Cove copper, Bell Island

iron ore
Down north, out west . . . wherever came the call
Gold in Nova Scotia, St. Lawrence . . . the mica
    mines in war . . ."

(He grasped his chest and struggled for his
    breath)
"Long hours . . . day after day . . . your body . . .
    worn . . .
There was no safety then . . . you lived with death
The dust . . . the damp . . . the way your lungs are
    torn . . ."

He paused again and looked into the fire
Searching there for all that he had lost
"The pay was good . . . not bad . . . the work was
    sure"
I thought I noticed bitterness creep in: "But b'y,
    the cost, the cost . . ."

He stood to catch his breath, then looked at me
Appealing, to make me understand
"I had to work . . . a wife and children . . . don't
    you see
There was no other way . . . that time . . . in
    Newfoundland"

ACROSS THE CHASM

"Come back from the dead! The most ridiculous thing I've ever heard. How can anybody come back from the dead? In all my years of medicine I've never heard such nonsense. Such inane drivelling nonsense. . . . Come back from the dead. . . . As if there were some place to come back from . . ."

Dr. Reilly's booming voice, its tone one of undisguised contempt, thundered in the near-silent oppressiveness of the packed lounge. Wearied patrons glanced with disinterest in his direction, then resumed their listless wandering about the room. Others stood in silence by the plate-glass window, totally oblivious to the conversation, their mood despondent as they gazed at the harsh March landscape outside. The sight of rime-coated trees, their mute forms sagging under the weight of so much frozen rain, their limbs broken and strewn about the dirty spring snow—detritus of the lingering winter—did little to uplift their spirits.

The worst sleet storm in living memory had grounded their plane at Gander, the bus chartered to take them on to St. John's had been forced to stop at the motel due to treacherous road conditions, and they had more on their minds than to listen to the self-importance of a voice that became more grating as the afternoon wore on.

185

Only the doctor's immediate listeners displayed any interest, but it was a reluctant interest, subdued in tone, uncomfortable as they were in the presence of his arrogant, bullish personality.

Pellets of ice rat-a-tatted an incessant drumbeat on the lounge window as Dr. Reilly continued, his contemptuous tone unchanged.

"People coming back. . . . The afterlife. . . . Literature and imagination. Great literature from a highly developed imagination . . . but only literature and imagination . . ."

Silence greeted his last remark. The priest moved to reply but seemed to think better of it. The public health nurse toyed with her glass, her eyes following its movements, while the company executive, his partially bald head pushed deep into his chair, slouched in the direction of the window, contenting himself with the incessant chewing of his nails. The government biologist, a rotund, genial little man with perpetual smiling face, fidgeted under the doctor's glare, feeling embarrassed that he had unwittingly started the argument by telling ghost stories.

Only Dr. O'Dea showed any real interest in rebuttal. She was a psychiatrist from Winnipeg who specialized in psychological disorders arising out of religious experience, and she welcomed any approach to the subject. She rested her arms on the table as she engaged Dr. Reilly, seemingly unperturbed by the overpowering force of his personality.

"But surely that literature and imagination has to have some basis in experience. Every primitive society since the emergence of the human race has expressed its concern with the afterlife and has shown all kinds of ways of expressing that concern . . ."

Dr. Reilly did not give her time to finish, making no attempt to disguise the sarcastic curtness of his reply.

"You are absolutely right, Dr. O'Dea. You are absolutely right. . . . How could such an eminent psychiatrist such as yourself be wrong?"

He then rose from his chair, his demeanour assuming a look of deep reverence—a look that did not hide the smirk that was forming at the corner of his mouth or the disdain and sarcasm that remained in his voice. He swung his empty brandy glass outward in a great, sweeping arc, parodying the act of delivering a toast.

"To the afterlife, ladies and gentlemen. . . . And to all the great civilizations who found their own ways of expressing it. To the pharaohs who sailed their immortal boats across the sky; the Norse who slaughtered valiantly for Valhalla; those ancient Indo-Aryans who gave us the Vedas and reincarnation; and all those wonderful Scythians who buried their dead with horses and spears . . ."

He sat down again, sweeping his eyes over the company as he set his glass on the table with a derisive clunk, the smirk now clearly visible.

"Literature, Dr. O'Dea. . . . Literature. Literature and imagination. Beautiful literature and beautiful imagination, but still literature and imagination. As I said at the beginning, the whole idea . . . the whole concept . . . is preposterous. There is no life after death. . . . There is no afterlife. There is no place to come back from. And even if there were, there is no evidence that anyone has ever come back . . . ever."

He relaxed his grasp on the glass and leaned forward, certain that the argument was over. He pronounced the next words with deliberation, the rhythmic beat of his finger on the table in accompaniment to each measured phrase.

"I repeat. No one has ever been known to come back. . . . No one has ever come back. . . . No one . . ."

Nothing was said in reply. A deep silence had settled over the group, a silence broken only by the incessant drumming of frozen pellets on the windowpane, an unnerving sound rendered more acute by the ominous flickering of the ceiling lights. The silence ended with the quiet intrusion of another voice, the voice of a tall, athletic-looking young man at the bar.

"But what if you are absolutely wrong . . . which is admittedly a possibility."

The voice emerged from the shadow of the bar as the form of the speaker materialized in front of the table.

"What if somebody would return, somebody you recognized? . . . Appear to you right in front of your face, so to speak. . . . Would you accept it then?"

Dr. Reilly turned, a contemptuous retort forming on his lips, but he visibly softened when he beheld the younger man who was the source of the questions. He recognized the speaker as another travelling companion from Toronto.

"Wrong, James?" He laughed. "Why, has somebody returned to you?" he added in a sly tone, winking in the direction of the government biologist.

The brandy was beginning to have its effect, and he again raised his empty glass in a toasting gesture, swinging his torso to face each member of the group in turn. The priest leaned back to avoid the moving arm.

"Let's drink again, gentlemen—and ladies—to my friend James and his guest from across the chasm. Standing before you is the absolute and living proof that I am entirely and unquestionably wrong . . ."

He then paused to set the glass on the table, restraining a chuckle as he ended on a humourously sardonic note.

". . . in the event that he should disappear into a cloud of smoke or brimstone or sulphur or whatever and our last piece of evidence will be lost forever."

The younger man moved quietly toward the table, unperturbed by the doctor's offensive tone.

"No, there were no clouds of smoke or brimstone or anything like that. There was none of that stuff . . . but I was there when it happened. And it wasn't me. I was just a witness, if you will. It had all to do with my friend Martin . . . and the return of his father."

His statements were uttered with such candour, such sincerity, that even Dr. Reilly, who up to now was shaking his head bemusedly, and quietly laughing in a condescending manner, stopped to listen.

The priest had motioned for the speaker to join the group, and they stood shuffling in various forms of movement to accommodate the chair which he was inserting into the ring of chairs around the small table.

He continued talking while he adjusted himself, setting his beer bottle on the table as he assumed the position of attention in their midst. The frozen pellets of rain continued their incessant fusillade on the window, trying to penetrate to the inside.

"I grant you, I never believed in that sort of thing myself, either . . . prior to what happened, that is. I mean, I'd heard lots of ghost stories growing up . . . stories about fairies taking children and leading people astray in the woods and that sort of thing. There was even an old abandoned house up the road that was supposed to be haunted. The old people frightened us to death when we were small with stuff like that. But when you grow up you realize that they were just that, stories, like Dr. Reilly was saying . . ."

Dr. Reilly smiled at the unexpected recognition, but then quickly resumed his skeptical look. A different mood now pervaded the listeners as they focused their full attention on the new voice. People at the surrounding tables ceased their conversations and turned to listen, and a lone drinker at the bar also turned to look in the speaker's direction.

"I was never much of a believer, if you know what I mean. Like a lot of people today, that stuff got thrown out the window as soon as I got big enough to stop going to church. Standing by a pond flicking in trout on a Sunday morning was a whole lot better than listening to somebody beating his gums in a pulpit. I wasn't the overly religious type."

"I expected you to talk about Martin."

The public health nurse was speaking in a tired tone, which didn't seem to perturb the speaker in any way, continuing in the easy tone with which he had begun.

"And I will. Because it was through my friendship with Martin that I came to experience what I did . . ."

The speaker paused to sip his beer, seemingly lost in himself.

". . . We were the best of friends . . . the best of friends . . . even though he was totally different . . ."

"Different?"

The priest turned his gaze from the window to focus on the speaker.

"Totally. I mean, Martin, to quote the old people, lived in the church. He had to be one of the more religious persons I have ever met. Said his morning prayers, said his evening prayers, said something called the Angelus at noon. . . . And this in the middle of a camp full of construction workers who weren't all that shy about poking a bit of fun. . . . Yes, he took his religion very, very seriously, that boy. Religion with a capital 'R', my uncle Jim would say . . ."

The speaker shook his head, smiling at the memory.

". . . Praying, reading those books. . . . I mean, I used to make the height of fun of those books. Could you imagine when you were seventeen or eighteen reading something called *The Pillars of Grace* . . . when there was all that other good stuff on the shelves . . . ?"

The speaker blushed as he detected a frown of condemnation from the priest, and hastened to continue.

"I mean, Martin didn't seem to mind. He would smile and say, 'James, I'm going to convert you yet,' and he'd go away shaking his head and laughing himself. Which he did a lot before his breakdown . . ."

"Breakdown?"

Dr. O'Dea was instantly alert, her physical motion attracting the attention of the speaker.

"That's what I calls it, anyway. I mean, he didn't wind up in hospital or anything like that . . . but just like that, when he struck nineteen he changed completely, like black and white. Before he was quiet, funny now and again. . . . After, the only word you could use to describe him was pitiful . . ."

Here the speaker stopped to motion to the passing waitress, pointing to his empty bottle. Within moments she had deposited another beer on the table as he continued speaking.

"I mean, Martin had always been the nicest kind of a person. But that summer when we went together as labourers on that big hydro construction job at Larch Falls—working our way through, you know—man, he changed . . . and I mean 'changed.'"

"How? How did he change?"

It was Dr. O'Dea again, leaning ahead with an expression of keen interest.

The speaker rested his arm on the table as he grasped his beer bottle, staring at it as if into a crystal ball of the past.

"I don't know. . . . Moody. . . . Far away. . . . Really sad. . . . Like he was in another world. You'd see him by himself just staring ahead at nothing at all. I mean, he kept his work up and all that, but he'd go for days and not speak. . . . Totally within himself. . . . And if it's possible to become more religious, he did it. Leave after work and go for hours in the bush. . . . I followed him once and found him sitting on a rock by the Larch River . . . praying, would you believe . . ."

"That isn't such unnatural behaviour," interrupted the priest. "The great mystics would spend days, weeks, in such solitary contemplation."

"But what brought all of this on?" Dr. O'Dea's eagerness was undisguised. "There must have been some traumatic upheaval in his life to affect his emotions like that."

The speaker lifted his gaze from the beer bottle to look directly into her eyes.

"I asked him that very thing. And after a while he told me. We were strolling along the bank of the Larch River one Sunday afternoon. Martin seemed to have come out of himself a bit, and when I kind of got after him to tell me what was wrong, he looked at me with the saddest expression you could ever see on a man's face. Then he looked at the river for a long time, like he was lost in the churning of the water. When he looked back he said: . . .

"'You want to know what is wrong with me, James? Would you understand if I told you? It's my father, James,' he said. 'My father.'"

"He was being abused by his father!" The public health nurse was not as shocked as she seemed quietly angry.

"Oh, no, nothing like that," the speaker replied. "That was impossible. Martin's father had died before he was even born. . . . Drowned off the Virgin Rocks. . . . You remember, that time the *Lucy Gray* went down with all hands. . . . While Martin was in the womb, so to speak."

"What's all this got to do with 'coming back'?"

It was the first time the company executive had spoken, and his sulkiness was apparent.

The speaker continued, ignoring the rudeness of the tone.

"Everything. Because my story is about Martin and his father. And because I don't think things like this happen to people like me and you. I think they only happen to people like Martin, people who really believe."

The man at the bar took advantage of the pause to sneer in the speaker's direction.

"I knew a buddy like that. He was always talking to God. Off his head . . ."

This attempt at censure was greeted by disapproving facial expressions around the table. Not expecting such a show of support for the storyteller from his audience, the man at the bar withdrew from the conversation, struggling with embarrassment.

"What I meant was . . . he was religion-crazy. The hospitals are full of people like that . . . delusions, hallucinations, seeing stuff like angels. . . . Isn't that so, Doctor?"

He had appealed to Dr. Reilly for support, but the doctor merely nodded assent and continued his focus on the speaker, who turned toward the man at the bar, eyeing him across the distance.

"I suppose. . . . I really don't know enough about that side of it. Although Martin didn't seem to be any of those things. Like I said, his work was never a problem, and when it was all said and done—in spite of all the tormenting—he got along pretty good with the men."

"So, in your opinion, he wasn't mentally unstable in any way."

Dr. O'Dea was pursuing the line of questioning she had begun.

"Not as far as I could see. He was pretty hung up about

his father's death. . . . Like he really missed him after all those years, although he had never, ever seen him. Over and over he'd say: 'If I could only see him just once, James. If I could only hear him speak to me just once. If I could only stand beside him on this riverbank. . . . Oh, James, how I have prayed to see him . . . just once. . . .' It was like he was in a continual search back in time for the father he never had."

"That would certainly explain the moody behaviour, the introspection," mused Dr. O'Dea. "Our latest studies show that the child in the womb can have maintained a form of liaison with the external parent."

She was speaking in a clinical manner, reviewing reports in her mind, as the speaker continued.

"He wasn't helped much in all of this by his mother, poor soul. Instead of helping the boy accept and overcome his father's death, she continually fostered his sense of belonging and loss."

"I suppose she was so devastated by the father's death."

The public health nurse had dropped her tired tone and was shaking her head in sympathy.

"Totally," replied the speaker. "She never recovered. Especially when the body was never found. She still continued on with her life in a more or less normal way, but she lived in the past, reliving over and over the two short years of marriage to her husband.

"She never accepted his death, and she constantly talked about him, night and day. . . . Story after story about her husband, Martin's father. And it wasn't just her. It seemed everybody had a good word to say about that man. Seems he was quite a person. As a result, Martin became totally caught up with wanting to see his father . . . in the living flesh, so to speak . . ."

"But he was dead. This is so irrational . . . so . . . sick."

The public health nurse was contorting her face disapprovingly.

"Perhaps. But you have to understand the longing that Martin—and his mother—were experiencing, and their conviction that the person who was such an important part of their lives was now living in another life . . . another world . . . right now . . . that he could be seen if one, say, believed enough, prayed enough . . ."

The speaker seemed to weaken as he detected a look of displeasure on Dr. Reilly's face.

"This is not terribly convincing," observed Dr. Reilly drily. "It's like I've said all along. Religion warps the mind . . . tremendous traumatic effects . . ."

"Sheer obsession," snorted the company executive. "I thought you said he was mentally stable."

"Please go on," insisted Dr. O'Dea, seeking to return the conversation to its original tone. "I find this very interesting. They actually believed they could somehow see him . . ."

"Yes," the speaker replied in her direction, detecting her professional interest. "They believed that this other world—this spirit world, if you will—was going on right around them. . . . That the people in this other world were very close and all you had to do was . . ."

"Set up a seance and get a medium," snorted the company executive.

The company executive shrunk back in embarrassment as the group again turned with disapproving looks.

The speaker continued, but his tone was awkward.

". . . was pray hard enough. He had picked up something about 'crossing the chasm' from one of those stories in the Bible, and he would use that phrase over and over. . . . 'If Dad could only cross the chasm' . . ."

"So on this side," interjected the priest, "one lives in a physical dimension, animated by a spiritual soul . . . then the soul moves at death to the spiritual dimension, kept from earthly communication by a chasm of some kind, as it is described biblically. That's pretty traditional Church teaching."

The priest was illustrating by holding his hands parallel and moving them definitively first to the left, then to the right. The speaker responded eagerly, totally unperturbed by the mild condemnation.

"That's exactly how he used to talk. About a chasm of some kind. He was always praying for his father to 'come across the chasm.'"

"A fourth dimension." Dr. Reilly sounded amused. "That's really not a very innovative idea, you know, old man. That was in the comic books when I was a youngster. It's still basically literature and imagination and not really very convincing."

His tone was one of a man who has suddenly lost interest in what up to now had been a rather good conversation, and was displeased to have been let down. The speaker turned in his direction, still unperturbed.

"No. With Martin it wasn't literature or imagination, or simple, shallow belief. He had thought about it continually, and was convinced, like his mother, that if he prayed and wished hard enough, it would happen one day, somewhere, sometime."

"So one night he saw his father, and has been talking about it ever since . . ."

It was the company executive again. His tone seemed to be becoming more terse and rude. The public health nurse was just as dismissive as she shrugged her shoulders.

"It could be simple wish-fulfillment. Put enough pressure

on a mind, especially a sensitive religious mind, as his obviously was, and it will hallucinate . . ."

"Yes," the priest agreed. "In South America there are numerous stories of women who claim to see apparitions. . . . They cause terrible problems for the Church."

"Okay. So you cross this side by the process of death," interjected Dr. O'Dea, still eager to listen. She was open to any knowledge or any new approach with which she could help her patients and had become totally engrossed in the narrative.

Her brow furrowed as she pieced together the structure of the thinking painstakingly in her mind.

". . . that doesn't prove you can cross in return. Let's say you can go from the physical to the spiritual; it still doesn't prove you can come back."

"Exactly as I said in the first place," muttered Dr. Reilly.

"Not as far as Martin was concerned," James replied, ignoring the doctor's comment. "Which brings me to my story."

"I thought that was the story."

The public health nurse looked bewildered.

"To me it's all bunk," shrugged the company executive, turning abruptly away from the company in a final gesture of contempt. The public health nurse glowered at him and started to say something, but she changed her mind. Dr. O'Dea nodded encouragingly to the speaker.

"Please go on. I'm anxious to hear the end."

"They don't come back." Dr. Reilly's tone was emphatic, but he seemed to have directed the statement to himself. "But tell us the story. Anything is an improvement . . . and it looks like we're going to be here for the day, anyway."

The wind had risen, rattling the window with a new round of sleet pellets.

"More than an improvement," adjoined the younger man. "The story will be proof of sorts that . . . that you are wrong."

197

"Proof!" snorted the doctor. "How can a story like this be proof? It's the blind following the blind . . . or the ludicrous following the ludicrous."

"Tell the story," came the quiet authority of the government biologist.

The speaker looked around the group and, satisfied that he had their attention sufficiently, began to narrate, in a clear, earnest voice.

"As I have said, I became acquainted with Martin in university in St. John's, and it was from St. John's that we set out that afternoon in March to head for Square Harbour, a little outport across the Silver Mountain River, two miles beyond Isle au Glu. Jamie Osborne had an old house out there belonging to his father, who had moved to Sudbury when his sawmill went out of business in the '50s.

"He and his girlfriend, Marina, had planned to spend the weekend there, so they invited the three of us—me, Martin, and Bill Lawton—to spend the weekend with them. The boarding houses were getting a bit monotonous that time of year, and a weekend having a beer and listening to Bill Lawton play the guitar sounded like a good idea, so we took them up on it.

"Martin didn't seem too eager to come with us at first—he had come down with one of those cursed moods again—but Marina talked him around, and we agreed we would leave as soon as possible after the one o'clock class on Saturday . . . to get a head start on the bay road. I mean, that road is bad enough in summer. . . . Marina was worried about the weather forecast, too.

"Although it was raining steady for three days, the weatherman was forecasting a change with snow—and we knew it would be no fun plowing snowdrifts in Jamie's old '56 Chev around the bay road. Like I said, Marina was worried, but the rest of us weren't paying any attention to it, knowing enough about Newfoundland weather and Newfoundland weather forecasts, and the fact that very rarely did the two ever get along . . ."

He stopped to let his group appreciate the humorous reference, but his listeners maintained an uninterrupted serious posture.

"We didn't get under way as early as we wanted—it was four o'clock and we were still packing—but it was still raining, so we weren't particularly worried about the weather. But as we set out from the city, Martin, for some reason, seemed to become really afraid.

"Granted, in the beginning he didn't show much interest, but his spirits seemed to rise in the fun of getting ready—packing food for Bill Lawton was a party in itself. However, as we left St. John's and headed out the bay road, he sunk back into his previous mood and seemed to become even more and more fearful, which was unusual. I mean, when he got into one of those moods, he would become as quiet as a mouse, and get really down, but I had never known him to exhibit fear."

"Perhaps with the weather forecast and the threatening weather conditions . . ." volunteered the government biologist.

"Perhaps. But he had driven with Jamie before in bad weather and he had every confidence in him. Jamie had the reputation of being one of the best winter drivers around, and he always kept his car in top shape. . . . And he never drank when he was driving. That was his unstated rule. So there was nothing to fear on that score on anybody's part. Besides, even the rain had stopped as we left the city, and like I said, nobody paid any attention to the weather forecast, anyway."

"Maybe he was just being Martin, if you know what I mean . . ." It was Dr. O'Dea volunteering this time.

"That's what we thought, but why he was so much in dread this time was beyond us completely, and we tried everything we could to shake him out of it. I mean, this time he was more than moody. He was eerie. He did eventually agree to go along with us, but his mind seemed to be somewhere else."

The speaker stopped to imbibe a long draft of beer, something he hadn't done for some time.

"We sat him between myself and Bill in the back, and Marina talked to him over the front seat. But nothing seemed to work. Martin just shrank farther within himself, shaking his head and retreating behind that vacant set stare which was his typical defence when being pressed in company.

"Bill Lawton had no patience with him at all and would curse at him in his good-natured way—'For the luvva. . . . Martin, lighten up, b'y. Put a smile on your face. I'll pay for the stitches'—but all to no avail. Martin just continued to sit there, staring straight ahead, with as down a look on his face, sir, as you could get.

"The only time when he showed any appreciation for our concern was when Jamie suggested out loud that perhaps it wasn't such a good idea and that maybe we should turn back. At that point, Martin seemed to come out of himself, reassuring us that he was fine now and that we should go on."

The speaker adjusted his position, smiling softly as he relaxed with the memory.

"Well, it didn't take long to get back to jokes and fun once we felt Martin was part of us again. After all, we were young and foolish, without a care in the world. Exams were coming up, but they were still a week away, and besides, like I said, this was the weekend. We were a good group and we always had fun together, but it didn't take long for things to change."

"Martin?" interjected Dr. O'Dea.

"No, the weather," replied the speaker, with a wry look on his face. "We were driving along, everybody except Jamie with a beer bottle in his hand, singing all kinds of old songs, not paying much attention to what was going on in the world around us . . .

"We hadn't noticed the dead stillness in the air or the little flicks of hail popping off the windshield and the bonnet of the car. That should have warned us that she was chopping off—that the temperature was dropping off really fast—rain turning to ice and snow."

He had spoken in Dr. O'Dea's direction when he had noticed she had a puzzled look on her face.

"When we left Croucher, just as we climbed onto the Mizzen Barrens,"—he talked as if his listeners were familiar with the route he was following in his mind—"you know where the track runs along the old abandoned talc mine, the storm hit us. And folks, she was a doozy. As the old people used to say, she socked in pretty fast.

"That's really high, open country out there, and the northeast wind just blew straight in off the bay, burying us in nothing less than a howling blizzard. To quote my uncle Jim Cassidy, the weatherman had told us we were going to have a 'starm,' he just never told us what kind of 'starm.'"

"Why didn't you just wait it out, or turn around and go back to the place you had left . . . Croucher?" asked the public health nurse.

"We debated that," the speaker replied, "but we felt we had no choice but go on. To stop and try to turn around might mean getting stuck right there on the barrens—and the Mizzen Barrens was no place to be stuck in a snowstorm.

"There wasn't a house or a cabin the entire twelve-mile stretch, and you might as well be stuck on Baffin Island. Tom Morey got caught like that three years before, and his wife and youngster almost died from exposure. Being young—and stupid—we felt safe so long as we were plowing through.

"Like I said, Jamie was the best kind of driver, and the

heavy Chev was pushing her way through the drifts well enough. Besides, we knew—if we could keep going—that it wouldn't be long before we were across the Barrens and going down the other side into the lun—the shelter—of the Silver Mountain River valley.

"We figured if we made it to the bridge, we were safe. The grade slopes downward on the lee side of the barrens—there was less chance of getting stuck—and if we did get stuck on the sloping side of the Barrens, we could survive it. Like I said, we would be more sheltered, we were rigged for the weather, and if we had to walk to Isle au Glu, it wasn't that far. Visibility hadn't gotten any worse, and we knew we were close to the black cliff of the Cut, which was the end of the Barrens and the beginning of the grade down to the bridge."

He stopped as if he were mentally peering into the distance.

"So we plowed along, trying to help out Jamie as best we could by peering through the blinding swirls of snow, keeping an eye on the sides of the road, especially when we approached the Cut, which we knew would be really bad. By this time it was coming on dark, and we were the only car on the road in that howling frenzy—everybody else had better sense.

"There were no lights of any kind, and, like I said, there were no houses or cabins. Certainly, if there were, it wouldn't have made any difference, since the storm had knocked out the power all along the coast and the houses would be in darkness, anyway."

"But you didn't get stuck?" There was a worrisome tone in Dr. O'Dea's voice.

"No, we didn't," the speaker replied. "We got through the Cut no problem—it wasn't as bad as we thought it was going to be—and we became more relieved as the car dipped downwards to the lower levels of the river valley. It was still a blinding snowstorm, but somehow we felt safer as we descended to the lower country. Even if we were trapped there, we could wait it out in the car, and not be exposed to the deadly, colder winds of the upper barrens.

"The car seemed to move faster, as if it were in tune with our new mood. Maybe we would get to Square Harbour after all. Sprays of snow spewed left and right as Jamie navigated the sweeping curve that led to the bridge—he knew the road like the back of his hand—trying to make up a little of the time we had lost on the Barrens."

Here the speaker injected a cautionary tone, as his face assumed a serious, almost sombre expression.

"You had to be careful approaching the bridge, even in summer, since the road curved so sharply to avoid the cliff that the bridge always suddenly appears out of nowhere, even when you are expecting it. I mean, you know how they built stuff in those days. Just like that you're past the cliff, over the rise, and bang—you're on the bridge.

"Marina had always been really nervous about crossing the bridge—it was one of those old narrow ones built in the '20s—and we knew that, and we started singing a bunch of old stuff again so her mind wouldn't be on crossing . . ."

"Yes, once you were across the bridge, you were getting closer to Square Harbour . . ." observed Dr. O'Dea, mentally calculating the distance.

"Yes, and we were all anxious to get there. Jamie was keeping the car in second, plowing through the snow, braking her just enough to keep from sliding off the curve along the cliff, but keeping her fast enough to be able to take the rise before we hit the bridge.

"With that storm, he knew that snow would be built up on the bridge, so once over the rise, he would have to speed up so he wouldn't get stuck on the bridge itself. I mean, Marina was petrified enough just going across that bridge; if she got stuck on it in the middle of a snowstorm, she'd simply go berserk."

Here the younger man paused, as if he were forming a mental picture.

"Now, if you can picture this. We're going a bit slow around the curve along the face of the cliff so we won't slide off into the ditch. We sidled a bit, but the blackness of the rock face eased by harmlessly enough . . .

"Jamie lines her up, right ready to give her the gas to pop over the rise to the bridge, with no way to stop or slow down once we crested the top, with the bridge and the river just feet away . . .

"Like I say, Jamie was right ready to nail her, sir, into the rise, barrel her over the top and straight through the bridge to the other side . . . when Martin screamed."

Looks ranging from irritation to shock greeted the unexpected break in the narrative.

"He finally cracked," muttered the company executive. He hadn't intended the remark to be heard, and he fidgeted in an embarrassed manner. James continued as if he weren't interrupted.

"I mean scream, sir, like you've never heard a scream. He screamed this wicked, loud, vicious 'Stop the car! For God's sake, stop the car! For God's sake, stop the car . . . !'"

The speaker leaned forward, right into the centre of the group.

"Now you can imagine the effect this had on us, sitting in that car, tight as drums in the middle of a howling storm, eyes burned raw from the strain of peering into the dark and the snow, nerves strung out like piano wire from going through the storm . . .

". . . Imagine that scene, ladies and gentlemen . . . when Martin screams. He hadn't spoken a word all through the storm. Just sat there, locked within himself. And just like that, just like it seemed we were all going to crack under the strain . . . and he screams; this nerve-wracking, soul-wrenching scream that explodes in the car like . . . well . . . like a stick of dynamite or something . . ."

At this point the speaker leaned back.

"Of course, when Martin screamed 'Stop the car,' that's exactly what happened. The car stopped. Jamie got such a start that he put both feet on the brake at the same time and stalled her dead—standard transmission, you know—smacko in the snowdrift.

"If there had been ice on the road, we would have gone halfway across the Avalon Peninsula out in the woods. Marina smacked the side of her head on the windshield. Bill Lawton and myself, sitting as we were up toward the front seat looking, were pitched forward.

"I just spilled the bottle of beer I was holding, but Bill was just then taking a mouthful, and he smacked the bottle into his teeth. Martin wasn't paying attention to any of that. He was gripping the back of the seat with both hands, looking straight through the windshield, his face utterly distraught."

"He'd seen his father," muttered the company executive drily.

The rest of the group passed no notice of the remark, attuned as they now were to his manner of interrupting. They were still attentive, their faces expectant and alert.

"Exactly," replied the narrator. "That's why he screamed. When Jamie came to himself, he switched on the light in the inside of the car and whipped around to Martin. I thought he was going to tear Martin apart right there in the back seat, he was that mad. I've never seen Jamie that mad.

"But Martin just looked at him with the most tearful expression and said, 'You were going to run over my father. You were going to hit him. He was standing in the middle of the road.'

"Bill Lawton got really mad and started to curse. He grumbled something to Martin under his breath about 'being off his head,' and got out of the car, feeling his broken tooth.

"Then Bill must have felt remorseful, because he came back and poked his head in again to tell us he was going to look at the river for a while. We all knew he just wanted to cool down. Even Marina was pretty upset, pointing out to Martin in no uncertain terms how he could have put us all off the road.

"Martin didn't hear any of it. He just kept looking at us one by one—the biggest kind of tears in his eyes—and saying over and over, 'You were going to kill my father.'

"I can still see Marina shaking Martin by the shoulder over the seat. I have never seen her so mad, either.

"'But your father is dead, Martin . . . dead, for heaven's sake. He's been dead for nearly twenty years. Get a grip on yourself. He was dead before you were even born. For God's sake, aren't you taking this stuff a little too far?'"

"You should have chucked him out in the snow," commented the public health nurse. "Causing a scene like that in those circumstances."

James looked nonplussed.

"I admit that the thought crossed our minds. But Martin just continued in his pleading voice. He hadn't been in the storm, he said. It was summer, he said, and we were driving down some big wide road on the prairies, tearing along, he said, and his father was standing there right in the middle of the road holding up both hands for us to stop. And we were going to kill him."

"He was dreaming," commented the priest. "It's so simple, it's almost obvious. Given the mental anguish occasioned by the loss of his father, his constant preoccupation with wanting to visibly see his father—all fostered by his mother. . . . The pressures of the moment came together to induce hallucination . . . a simple dream."

"Exactly as I said at the beginning," called the man from the bar.

The listeners seemed to be on his side, their looks and gestures giving him more encouragement.

"I agree entirely," stated Dr. Reilly, totally disinterested.

"I must confess," Dr. O'Dea began very slowly, her tone somewhat crestfallen, "that I had hoped for something more illuminating . . . but I have to agree with Fr. Cowan. A type of wish-fulfillment under very arduous mental and emotional circumstances."

The government biologist said nothing.

The speaker was unaffected by this discourse.

"And that's what we would have thought, too, the rest of us in the car . . . until we saw Bill Lawton."

"How does Bill come into it," asked the company executive, suddenly interested.

"Well, like I said, Bill had gotten out to go stand on the bridge, to cool himself down after Martin's performance—which was unnerving, to say the least. Jamie had started the car again, to try to back her out, and, with the car lights shining directly ahead, the wind not as strong in the shelter, we could detect Bill's form on the rise over the river a short distance ahead.

"What caught our attention was the strange way Bill was walking, staggering like he was weak. I mean, Bill Lawton went through the snowdrifts in the woods like a bull moose in a panic. Then, while we watched, he grabbed the limb of a spruce for support and got as sick as a dog, retching right there in front of us.

"Bill Lawton would never do that."

"The exertion, the alcohol, the emotional upset, the close confines of the heated car. He was simply nauseous."

Dr. Reilly was making a clinical diagnosis.

"That ran through our minds—Jamie and I—as we jumped out of the car and ran to where he was, shouting to him over the storm, asking him what was wrong. He looked like he was going to pass out right there in the snow, and he practically fell into our arms when we got to him through the drifts.

"When he came to himself, he just pointed his arm in the direction of the bridge—he couldn't speak—and kept on vomiting. The way he was getting on really frightened us, and it took us a while to come up with the courage to look toward the bridge, not knowing what to expect. You know, where people hang themselves from bridges . . . there could have been a car ahead of us smashed into the railing, a body decapitated through the windshield . . ."

"What was it?" queried the public health nurse, unable to restrain her curiosity. "What did you see when you looked toward the bridge?"

An air of tension hung over the group as they collectively leaned forward in the speaker's direction, hanging on the speaker's next words.

The speaker's eyes rested on the group, his face seeming to reflect his own disbelief in memory.

"Well, that's it. We didn't see anything. When we looked where Bill was pointing, there was nothing. . . . Absolutely nothing."

Bewildered, puzzled looks greeted the announcement. The priest first broke the silence.

"Then, what made him so sick? What was he pointing at? What was on the bridge?"

The speaker paused and looked toward the window, a far-away look in his eyes, pondering the priest's questions.

"What was he pointing at? What had upset him? What did he see? . . . Nothing. At least nothing on the bridge. There could be nothing on the bridge . . ."

Here the speaker paused again as he struggled to relive the memory, trying to find a way to say the words that he knew would fall like a thunderclap in the eerie silence.

"There was no bridge. . . . Where the bridge was supposed to be—and I don't know if I can describe this for you—was a mad, surging, howling, cascading torrent of foaming water tearing along massive chunks of ice, beating them to pieces on the exposed boulders. . . . The bridge was gone . . ."

"What!"

A collective gasp emanated from the group, a sudden, resounding gasp that extended outward beyond the table, until it was lost in the relentless drumming of the sleet on the windowpane. From the stunned silence emerged the shocked voice of the public health nurse.

"But how . . . ?"

She did not finish. Like the rest, the unexpectedness of the statement had left her without words. The speaker continued in his matter-of-fact tone, twirling his half-empty beer bottle, absorbed in its motion as he spoke.

"Well, we had had all that rain which flooded the river. The mild weather and the current had broken up the ice in the backwaters, and it had all got dammed up somewhere back in the river. When the river burst through under all that pressure of ice and water, it just carried the bridge before it, like chips in a flood.

"Those old bridges weren't built as high as the new ones, and it was just swept away. Under the force of all that ice and water, it just didn't stand a chance. I heard later that they found pieces of it in Shoal Arm, ten miles downriver."

"In another minute . . . in another second . . ."

A look of horror had appeared on the nurse's face.

"You would have all been killed . . . the car and everybody in it would have simply disappeared into the river . . ."

Dr. O'Dea had finished the thought for her. Anybody else could have done it.

"Definitely," assured the speaker. "If Jamie had followed through, gunning the car over that rise into the last few feet of grade, the car would have been impossible to stop. . . . We would have had absolutely no chance."

"Except for Martin," observed the government biologist.

"Or his father," adjoined the priest.

"That's the way I see it," the speaker confirmed. "Martin prayed for his father to come back. And he did come back. But not just for any old reason. He came back to save our lives; whether as a dream, or a vision . . . or as a real person. If it weren't for Martin 'seeing,' I wouldn't be here today. So it is proof enough for me. Has anybody ever come back? I firmly believe Martin's father did."

The speaker stood and grasped his beer bottle as he headed in the direction of the bar. The group remained seated as they followed his movements, wrestling with the horror of what could have happened, and what to them was the mystery of the outcome. Only Dr. Reilly spoke, repeating the same words over and over.

"Great literature and great imagination. Great literature and great imagination . . ."

The bus driver appeared in the doorway, announcing that the bus was on the point of leaving. The group responded in a disorganized manner, shuffling about and donning topcoats and scarves.

The road past Maccles must be open," observed the government biologist. "Let's see if we can get the same seats."

Dr. O'Dea had turned in the direction of the speaker,

who was now standing at the bar in conversation with the waitress.

"What about Martin?" she called out over the din of movement. "You must have been very grateful to him."

"Very much so," replied the speaker, turning in her direction. "As we sat in the car overnight, we thought about what had happened a dozen times over. We never really apologized to Martin, but then it was like we didn't have to. Martin was a different man from that day on. He didn't crow or throw it up to us or anything like that. Martin wasn't that kind of person.

"He became a man, as they say, at peace. He seemed happy at the way things had gone, that he had truly and finally seen his father, that his father had come back to save our lives . . . that all he had ever believed and prayed for had been proven, so to speak, before our very eyes."

"What ever happened to him?" queried the public health nurse, adjusting her scarf as she spoke.

"I don't know," the narrator responded, frowning as he pursed his lips in thought. "I haven't seen him now since we graduated. The last I heard of him he was in one of those monasteries in western Canada."

Dr. Reilly was making his way around a chair, a very thoughtful look on his face.

"So, Dr. Reilly," asked Dr. O'Dea, smiling quietly as she nudged him. "Are you preparing a great rebuttal for James during the ride back?"

"No, no," he answered soberly, his tone quietly academic. "I will not attempt a rebuttal. I enjoyed the discussion . . . the story; but it is still, for me at least, in the realm of literature and imagination. I still don't believe. . . . I can't. To believe now would . . ."

He didn't finish. But then, he didn't have to, since they

all understood. He stood quietly and adjusted his topcoat, then proceeded to join the crowd moving haphazardly toward the exit. He walked past James, pausing just long enough to rest his hand upon the younger man's shoulder. Their eyes met as he passed, and it seemed as if they understood each other.

A "NOBLE" SPRUCE

You talk about cutting Christmas trees.

You should have been around the year my only teenage daughter wanted to cut her own Christmas tree. She wanted a "cut" tree instead of a "bought" one, which, in outport parlance, is something like the taste of "homemade" bread as opposed to "baker's."

Since my paternal ego couldn't take another beating in these recurrent father-daughter confrontations, I didn't get into the distinctions between "cut" and "bought" trees, or the fact that "bought" trees are only "cut" trees once removed—if you don't mind the pun.

She wanted, she said, to preserve "the ageless family tradition," which was her way of describing the three times I took her to cut the Christmas tree when she was a child. She was sixteen now and had inherited her mother's romantic approach to things, and she vividly remembered every detail of that first time I took her up to Barry's Grove on her first tree-cutting expedition.

She was a pudgy little thing swaddled in umpteen layers of winter clothes, and since she was too small to walk alongside, she sat astride my shoulders as I plowed through the almost impenetrable snowdrifts of the winding wood-path, sometimes up to my waist in the deepest snow we had since John Guy got frostbite.

We had had a ferocious early winter storm two days before, so the trees were laden with a fine, powdery snow, the kind that goes down in your neck and back very easily.

Whether or not she was aware of that in her childlike mind I will never know, but she took a particularly perverse delight in leaning forward and swatting the overhead branches under which we passed, squealing with delight at the clouds of dry, powdery stuff that engulfed her, and found its way with uncanny accuracy straight down the back of my neck.

As I struggled with me, her, and a sharp axe through some of the deepest snowdrifts since the second ice age, you can imagine that I wasn't having nearly as much fun as she or that, for me, the memories of the day would be as romantically captivating.

Now here we were, thirteen years later, with very different approaches to Christmas and Christmas trees, since there's nothing like cold snow down a warm spine in December to put the romantic past in a reality perspective. I was understandably more interested in instituting a more modern family tradition—like buying a Christmas tree on the side of the road from Bud Squires, a suggestion which was greeted on her part by profound adolescent shock.

In her view, I was definitely not a romantic person, and certainly not a Sagittarius, to even contemplate such a idea. Besides, even I knew Bud was hardly old enough, the way he did his hair was, well, "gross," and I suspected that spending ten minutes buying a perfectly good tree from Bud Squires paled in comparison to roaming the ridge on a beautiful sunny afternoon with the seventh, and most newly acquired boyfriend, who was "a definite hunk," and "so-o-o-o her."

Now being tough with my only teenage daughter rarely

resulted in the kind of positive bonding you see on the television shows these days, so I gave in and let her have her way.

It was just as well since her mother, who up to now had not intervened, decided that I had had enough role-playing experience as father for one day and paused in the middle of her cup of tea to quietly say "Now dear."

Which to anybody else was simply "Now dear" but was really mother to father talk for "She'll only be with us for a short time more and don't you think you should give in to her this once just for peace in the family and then it is Christmas and she is your only daughter and she loves you very much and you know you love her . . ."

Totally vanquished, I got my good axe and motioned over my shoulder to my only daughter in the direction of Barry's Grove. She stood rigid, totally appalled. Assuming that she mistook my action for something of more murderous intent, given our recent disagreement over the tree cutting, I assured her that it was necessary to take the axe in order to cut the tree, and that I never took these family spats that seriously.

"It's not that, Dad," she blurted in astonishment. "You're . . . you're coming with us!"

I think she would have preferred to have been sold into slavery.

Following the pattern established from similar engagements in the past, complete dismay followed astonishment as she declared, her voice shaking with disbelief:

"I *am* sixteen, you know."

The now-familiar pattern continued, dismay now being transformed into positive terror.

"If any of my friends saw me with you . . . I would . . . die," this last being uttered in a tone similar to that when the heroine collapses on the stage in a seriously dramatic play and the curtain closes to end the act.

Well, I didn't want her to die as the result of any silly old Christmas tree, so I handed her the axe, sighed in resignation, and tried to salvage what fatherly pride I could from the situation by preparing them for the expedition.

You talk about your ageless family traditions.

I led her outdoors, where the seventh definite hunk was leaning against the corner of the house waiting out our confrontation, none the worse for the half-acre of snow that had settled momentarily on his two-hundred-pound-plus frame, and proceeded to give them both careful instructions on how to choose a proper Christmas tree, just as my mother had done for me, when I was sixteen.

"It is imperative," I said, in the authoritative tone I had acquired as a director of education, "that it be a 'small' tree . . . and definitely 'fir,'" reverting to a more grammatically correct mode of conversation for more communicative effect.

I felt that by using "definitely" I could ease the generation gap, and I deliberately avoided pronouncing "varr" in the old Newfoundland way, because she was already in the middle of the new grade twelve program, which came from Alberta, and she wouldn't understand the word, anyway. While she shuffled impatiently, I emphasized my point by directing her to a small "varr" at the edge of the marsh.

With the help of a tape measure and a large triangular piece of plywood laid out on the lawn, I outlined the required dimensions, insisting on symmetrical proportions, all delivered in minute detail, in that exact same tone of voice I used as a teacher in Barker's Cove, when the grade ten class used to go to sleep.

My next-door neighbour looked at me for a long time

over the fence before resuming his own struggle with a timing chain in a small Toyota, but since we had tacitly agreed some years earlier to totally ignore each other's strange behaviours, he never said anything about my plywood Christmas tree and I never said anything about his timing chain.

I tried not to watch him out of the corner of my eye as I continued my listing of specifications and dimensions for the benefit of my only daughter and the seventh definite hunk, concluding my exhortation with a grandiose movement of my arms as the final confirmation of the shape of the tree I wanted cut.

That's when my next-door neighbour's head disappeared from view under the hood of the Toyota, his body convulsing uncontrollably. I couldn't make out if he was laughing or not, or I would have said something really nasty about his timing chain, so I chose to ignore the visibly shaking parts of his body as I continued, in my incredibly self-controlled manner—referring to the plywood shape one more time, just for emphasis.

With the seventh definite hunk now standing beside her, affectionately holding her hand and exchanging glances like those boy and cow moose in October, it is doubtful if the precision of the delivery was all that effective.

They were halfway across the marsh before they thought of the axe, and they had exhausted the third ice age before they even got to the big birch tree at the corner of the little river. As I watched them finally enter the grove, hand in hand, their slow steps intertwining, I hoped they wouldn't be found swooned to death in a snowdrift by the Tout.

When they finally disappeared into the path that led to the grove, I wondered what would people say if I had to decorate the tree at Easter.

They were gone a long time, but in the fashion of that famous general who left the Philippines at the beginning of the Second World War, they did return . . . two hours after dark. They were both exhausted, and were dragging a huge black spruce tree, tall enough to reach the top storey of the St. John's city hall, and thick enough at the base to hide it.

To make matters worse, they had lost my best axe.

They looked cold and wet, but exuberance at a job well done shone on both their tired faces, and I considered it prudent for the moment to make no comment on the considerable difference between what I had described, "what ought to be," and what had been dragged home, what really "was." If ever there was a contrast between the philosophic ideal and the philosophic real, it was lying there on my front lawn, and pretty well covering it from back to front.

Hypocritically hiding my feelings beneath a congratulatory smile, I motioned them into the warmth of the kitchen, where her mother had hot chocolate steaming in two big mugs. To loosely paraphrase Genesis, I gazed upon their handiwork, shook my head in disbelief, and went to bed.

The next day was Sunday, and, just after breakfast, my only daughter and I had "rings around," which is a way Newfoundlander's have of describing a great big fight. The seventh definite hunk hadn't arrived yet, so I could indulge in my full parental authority without the fear of the human equivalent of an oversized Newfoundland bull moose interfering on the other side.

I must say that it wasn't the calibre of the fights they used to have on the public wharf years ago, but it provided good entertainment for my next-door neighbour's wife, who followed all the fights on television and who had no intentions of missing one that promised to be the best one on the block in years.

She could hear the racket through the walls of both houses, so she raced across and settled herself comfortably on the
back steps, totally immune to the December cold in a thick
down-filled parka and very expensive sealskin boots. She had
missed the world championship heavyweight title fight in
August, so feeling that this one would do just as well, she settled herself away, and cheered for my only daughter the whole
way through.

As for my only daughter, since the big spruce was the first
one she and the seventh definite hunk had cut together, and
since they would "definitely" be going steady after Christmas,
she wanted it decorated as "the" Christmas tree.

I countered that it was impossible to decorate a Christmas
tree that stretched corner to corner across the living room. For
once her mother did not quietly say "Now dear," with its intimidating translation, but exited silently to the safety of the
dining room, preferring the comfort and solace of the little
corner television to the noise and racket of yet another father-
daughter confrontation.

Armed as I was with physical size, advancing age, and the
threat of never opening my wallet again, I slowly brought her
around to my way of thinking, at least on the surface.

It took every bit of knowledge I had acquired from the
three women I had dated in my lifetime to bring her around,
but I must have done a pretty good job. She agreed that the
spruce tree could become the outdoor tree. I approved of this,
since, once it was up, it would do an immensely better job of
hiding the peeling paint on the front of the house than prone
and rammed butt-end into my newly carpeted front porch
where she had defiantly vowed to leave it.

She didn't even seem to make a fuss when I suggested
buying an indoor tree from Bud Squires. How graciously
she accepted defeat in the long run, however, was open to

question. Bud gave us the best tree he had in his yard, and it came pretty close to filling my dimensions, but it seemed no amount of artistic or aesthetic form was going to replace the giant abnormality which lay sullen and rejected in my front entrance.

I put the newly acquired purchase in a bucket of sand and stood it in the corner, and she even offered to help me decorate it, although her tone was very suspicious. She just kept smiling sweetly and commenting on "my cute little varr" every time she thrust another ornament on a branch, and I knew that wasn't going to be the end of it.

Just as she placed the little green angel on the top of the tree, our big black-and-white cat—named Sugar in obvious disregard for the way he prowled around the house all day long snarling like a polar bear on a March diet—did something which I am convinced he could not replicate to this day.

Whether he had a momentary regression to the kittenhood that he had missed so desperately, or had simply been so inspired by all that television coverage of the Newfoundland summer games, I will never know. He leaped straight over the coffee table to smack a dangling ornament, landed snarling and spitting in the midst of all the icicles and decorations, and brought the whole works crashing down in the middle of the living room carpet, which, with my incredible efficiency, I had had the foresight to have thoroughly cleaned that very morning.

The little green angel came to earth headfirst, and I raised my eyes to heaven. How a cat that size ever mustered the energy and speed to make an Olympic-standard leap like that I will never know, but the way he winked at my only daughter as he exited flying through the back door, I swear she had him put up to it.

My wife appeared on the scene upon hearing the crash,

and I looked to her for sympathy and understanding, given my chaotic plight. However, her only reaction was a threatening frown and the second utterance of an intimidating "Now dear," which at this point could be roughly translated as "What are you doing now and don't you dare raise your voice to that little girl and if I find one mark on this furniture or one tear in this new carpet . . ." Which of course didn't speak well for the undying support of the traditional Newfoundland family in times of crisis.

Still, she pitched in, and between the three of us the little varr was set upright again. My only daughter helped, but I imagined I detected just the merest hint of a triumphant gleam in her eye from time to time. We then proceeded to extricate the big spruce from the front porch as a first step in having it erected on the lawn as the outdoor tree.

This action on our part suddenly transformed my only daughter into the equivalent of a world federation wrestler. She grabbed the tree by the top and, with a snatch that would have done credit to a Siberian weightlifter, yanked it free of the porch door, darn near taking the door jamb with it.

She then dragged it and me down the front steps and across the patio to the hole I had prepared for it earlier in the fall, or at least toward a hole I had prepared for a much smaller tree. I had to do a lot of chopping on the butt end with a blunt axe and pour buckets of hot water into the frozen hole to make it small enough to fit, but we finally managed to force in the trunk and stand the behemoth up straight.

It took us a number of hours, a lot of lights, and a very long ladder to decorate our colossus, but we finally succeeded. Cars going up and down the harbour slowed down, and you could see faces gaping in amazement through the windows, but I couldn't hear them laughing, so I didn't mind.

Except for Bill Kearney.

He yelled something about getting a couple of Light and Power linesmen, but I couldn't understand what he was talking about so I ignored him, which is what you got to do with Bill, anyway. I must say that when we flicked the outdoor switch and, as they say, "she" lit up, "she" didn't look that bad. I mean, it was big, but what's wrong with a big tree?

It wasn't like that fellow in the 'States with the million Christmas lights and everybody complaining. It wasn't like that at all. My next-door neighbour said that he bet it would look really good from the Lookout, which is over a mile away, but he's not like Bill Kearney.

I did get one call, and the more I think about it, the madder I get. It was the next night, the night before Christmas, like in the poem. A very serious-sounding person called from Torbay airport—at least he said he was from Torbay airport—and he told me he had something very important to tell me and would I be prepared to give him my fullest co-operation.

Since he sounded very official, and since he told me he was over all the other air traffic controllers, I naturally listened to him and promised I would do what I could, like he asked. He said that according to his calculations, my outdoor Christmas tree was right under—that is directly under—the flight path of the big jets coming in from Gander.

"Mr. McCarthy," he said very politely, "we just received a call from the pilot of flight 763 from Toronto, Ottawa, and Halifax. Your Christmas tree lights are obscuring his approach to runway five, and he would appreciate it if you would turn them off for a moment so he can land safely. Confirm with me, will you?" and he held the telephone.

Well, I didn't want a big jumbo jet landing in my marsh just before Christmas—we only had one turkey and one dark fruitcake—so I went down right away and shut off all my outdoor lights.

Of course, I should have known that that pilot couldn't call from all those places at the same time, and that Torbay airport had only three runways. Still, it didn't strike me until I went back to the phone and heard someone tittering in the background that my cousin Bob Foley is ticket agent with that outfit and that, as they say in Newfoundland, they were having a game with me. No doubt he put them up to it all along, although he never admitted it.

You could say that we had the brightest Christmas ever that Christmas. We lit up both trees faithfully every evening, and I sat in the living room with my wife admiring my little varr, while my only teenage daughter and the seventh definite hunk would stand outside on the lawn admiring what my stepfather would have called "a noble spruce."

And what's wrong with having two trees, anyway?

"It's not like having two women, is it?" I said to my wife jokingly.

She glowered and gave me that look which could be interpreted as "I'll kill you first—then her," and I rushed to get her a quick cup of tea.

At that point my next-door neighbour and his wife joined us for a first Christmas visit, and we all agreed that we would have a hot toddy to toast the holiday season. As if by some telepathic prior agreement, he didn't mention my plywood shape and I didn't mention his timing chain, and his wife didn't mention the fight, although I heard after Christmas that she had spent a lot of time congratulating my daughter on the way in.

Women stick together like that.

We all agreed that smaller trees are better than bigger trees, anyway, and only somebody like Bill Kearney would have a big tree in his living room. My next-door neighbours are always on side when it comes to discussing the really important stuff.

With her seventh definite hunk and her very first Christmas tree together in the same spot, my only daughter forgot about our fight, and I made a mental note to forget about the snow down my back. So, to some degree, we both lived happily ever after.

Time and good feeling have a way of eradicating most bad memories, and making the present ones look downright appealing.

As for Bob Foley, he can't fool me. I knew he was behind it all along.

ONE SMALL BOOK

Books to read—when I went to school—there
    was a woeful lack
Except the few you carried in a denim bag upon
    your back
There were no fancy libraries with rows of books
    stacked shelf by shelf
And lots of times you had no money to buy a
    book yourself

Oh, the teachers tried as best they could to teach
    a dozen grades
(I tried it once and I tell you, sir, they deserve
    their accolades)
But even when they did their best, books were
    hard to find
Ah, there was lots to do for the body back then,
    but precious little for the mind

But in this tale of dark and woe, there is a ray of
    light
It's all about a book I got, a book that came one
    night
It was down among some well-packed clothes,

beneath a pair of skates
A book that came from far away, in a barrel from
the 'States

For in the town where I grew up, lots of folks had
gone away
To climb steel in Boston and New York, to find
a better day
And when things improved for them, when
prosperity they'd find
They'd send back barrels of clothes and things to
us who stayed behind

'Twas in one such barrel I found this book, from
a cousin just as keen
As I was for reading, a boy I'd never seen
They'd buy lots of books for him, and when he'd
read them through
He'd send them off to Harbour Main so I could
read them, too

Well, you may depend I was the happiest boy
you ever met
A brand new book, all mine to keep, you may
say, sir, I was set
I stole away to a quiet spot, to escape the kitchen
noise
To that mysterious house upon the cliff, with
those sleuths, the Hardy Boys

Many a happy hour I spent with Frank and Joe,
and their chubby buddy Chet
And except for the fact that life goes on I think

I'd be there yet
Ah, the mystery—the excitement—with each
chapter that I read
The dreams I had of solving crimes each night I
went to bed

Well, I must have read that book a thousand
times, deaf to the world outside
Then I took my precious book to school, to show
it off with pride
You should have seen them gather 'round, beg-
ging for a look
I was the star of the classroom show with my
brand new mystery book

At recess the teacher read the book to faces rapt
in awe
There wasn't a stir or movement, sir, the quietest
class you ever saw
When the bell would ring and 'twas back to
work, many a face would scowl perplexed
They'd have to wait another day to hear what
happened next

Well, pretty soon that book was read by every
girl and boy
Could you imagine that one small book could
offer so much joy?
We searched for Bayport on a map (For us this
fiction stuff was new
So convinced we were that the story of the Hardy
Boys was true)

Our teacher was so impressed with our love for
    Frank and Joe and Chet
That she had a concert and raised some money
    and bought the entire set
When the girls complained of being left out—
    Well, they were readers, too
She promptly mailed a cheque away for—you
    guessed it—"Nancy Drew"

With all those books passed hand to hand the
    room was pretty quiet that year
Pages turned—sighs of delight—the only sounds
    you'd hear
Even the lads down in the back, who made most
    of the noise
As quiet as mice around the cat—when reading
    the Hardy Boys

They all left school and went their ways to begin
    their lives for real
The girls to be secretaries on the base, the boys
    to work at steel
I'd meet them and they'd talk of books and of
    how their school days really flew
How their love of reading and books began with
    the Hardy Boys and Nancy Drew

I don't guess my cousin will ever get thanks
    enough for the fantastic thing he'd done
The reading he brought into our lives, the excite-
    ment, the downright fun
No, he'll never get thanks enough for that mar-
    vellous step he took

He got us reading night and day by sending . . .
    one small book

Acknowledgements

I would like to thank Shelley Chase of Garrison Hill Entertainment for her technical direction and assistance; Joan Tubrett for her reading of the final manuscript and invaluable advice; all those storytellers over the years who have provided me with such inspirational material, notably my brother George Furey and my brother-in-law, Bill Whelan; and lastly my wife, Eleanor, for initial critiquing of my work and for her continued support and encouragement.

It started with a comical tale about raisin bread, baked in an outport kitchen without raisins. Today, Hubert Furey has been more surprised than anyone by what has followed for him. The outpouring of interest for his recitations about rural life in yesteryear Newfoundland and Labrador led to a full-length recording of stories. Concerts, live theatre performances, television and radio appearances promoting recitations, and the resurgence of the art form have been a delight for this former district superintendent of education and lifetime Harbour Main resident. Hubert and his wife, Eleanor, have five children and six grandchildren. *As the Old Folks Would Say* is his first book.